Police Pranks

&
Misdemeanors

Wyatt Holmes

Police Pranks & Misdemeanors

Copyright © 2014 by Wyatt Holmes

ISBN: 978-0-9885902-9-8

Library of Congress: 2014934028

La Maison Publishing, Inc.

www.lamaisonpublishing.com

Prologue

Police officers love to play practical jokes. This is probably true for all first responders who through no fault of their own witness sights, sounds and situations which no reasonable person should have to experience. It's clear that jokes are just one of the coping mechanisms used by police officers to help them deal with their day to day activities on the street, at the office, or in the courts. Most police jokes are played on fellow law enforcement personnel; however, sometimes a situation is such that one or more "clients" end up being the brunt of such antics. Occasionally, as in any walk of life, police practical jokes skirt a fine line between innocent pranks and some level of illegal behaviour, however minor; hence the inclusion of "misdemeanors" in the title of this collection of anecdotes.

For obvious reasons, the names of persons and places have been changed to protect the innocent, or the guilty; whichever the case may be. The limitation of action for most reported misdemeanors should have long since expired, but just in case the author has erred on the side of caution in this respect. The author has also taken a certain amount of literary license in preparing these short stories for publication. While some stories are hearsay, the majority are presented as firsthand accounts; again, with slight modifications to protect the status, standing, secrets, and sanity of those directly involved.

Of course, the author may have made up all of these anecdotes out of thin air—an exercise in pure fiction. You be the judge. One way or the other, the author hopes you enjoy these stories.

Assault by "person or persons" unknown

Like most police academies, ours was run like a military camp. We had a nightly curfew and a guardhouse to ensure all cadets reported back in on time after a well-deserved night out on the town. One night the guard room really came alive when a cadet returned from downtown with his face, hands and clothing literally ripped to shreds! He stumbled into the guard room in considerably less than a sober state, so had considerable difficulty explaining his spectacular appearance.

That evening's Supervising Instructor was quickly called and after cursory inspection of the cadet was ready to call out the local police and perhaps the rest of the academy to track down the person or persons unknown who had inflicted such grievous bodily (and sartorial) harm to our fellow cadet. However, just as the wheels of revenge were about to be put in motion, our drunken friend sobered up enough to mumble his story to the astonishment of everyone present. During the year in question, a new building was under construction which necessitated special access for materials and heavy machinery. As a result, a section of ten-foot high barbed wire fencing had been rolled off of its posts and deposited in a heap alongside another section of still intact fence. Realizing that he was about to miss the standard curfew, the drunken cadet had run out of the bar he was in and flagged down a taxi. He told the driver to take him back to the academy as fast as he could. On arrival—just past curfew of course—he found the gate locked. So after paying off the taxi, the drunken cadet brazenly scaled the adjacent ten-foot high barbed wire fence. To save time, he jumped down on the other side into—you guessed it—the pile of rolled-up fencing, barbs and all! As he floundered around like a boozed-up beached whale, he received hundreds of tiny wire cuts to both body and clothing.

The cuts quickly healed and a new suit replaced the tattered and shredded garment the cadet wore that night. However, despite his best efforts, for the rest of his training he was not allowed to forget that particular night's misadventure. I'm sure that he still remembers today the night he was attacked by "wire or wires" unknown!

Time for a rumble—NOT!

Everyone's heard about hazing in military boot camps, college fraternities and other closed educational environments. Police academies are no different. At our academy, this phenomenon was often exercised in the form of a senior class raiding the dormitory of a junior class. Without warning, a horde of beefy bodies would fly into a dorm to flip over chairs, beds and anything else lying around. The object was to create chaos in another's dorm just before lights-out at 10:30 p.m. This meant that the invaded class would have to put everything back in place either in the dark or with the help of flashlights; and midnight inspections by instructors were common. It goes without saying that "lights out" meant just that and any class found with lights on after 10:30 p.m. or with their dorm in disarray, would find themselves washing out latrines or performing some other miserable or malodorous extra duty.

On one occasion, our class was lucky enough to get advance warning of a pending raid. We resigned ourselves to protecting our belongings as best we could. We got our mattresses at the ready so that the raiding class would have to run through our dorm striking mattresses instead of beds, bodies and everything else in their path. As we finished up our preparations we were surprised by an unexpected visit by a couple of grizzly old Sergeants. They were on an advanced training course and were billeted in single rooms adjacent to our dorm.

"Looks like you boys are preparing for trouble," one of the Sergeants remarked with a smile. "Expecting a raid are you?"

"Uh, yes Sir, sergeant," one of our mates replied. "We heard they was gonna hit us again just before lights-out. They hit us hard last time so we figured we'd be ready for them this time. We can't stop them (tradition forbid resisting, arguing or seeking retribution on a senior class), but we thought we'd give them a run for their money this time!"

"Don't call me 'Sir' boy," grinned the sergeant. "I work for a living! Whadda say, Hank, let's give these boys a hand tonight?"

"Sounds good to me," the other sergeant chuckled. "Get into bed boys, we'll take it from here!"

So we put our mattresses back in order and slipped under our covers—silence reigned. A short while later (around 10:15 p.m.), the sound of heavy boots hitting the stairs outside our dorm could be heard. When the raiding class burst through the double-doors at one end of our dorm they were met by the two grizzly sergeants in full dress uniform!

"Whoa back there young fellas!" said the larger of the two sergeants. "Can we help you boys any?"

Talk about a whole troop of cadets coming to a complete halt in short order; not to mention all the stuttering and stammering! The two sergeants then proceeded to give the would-be raiders a rather long lecture on the ethical behavior expected of cadets, especially senior cadets. They timed their lecture well; it ended at exactly 10:29 p.m., giving the senior cadets a mere 60 seconds to get back to their own dorm before "lights-out."

Although devoid of any power to actually punish the invaders, our visiting sergeants certainly put the fear of God into the senior class that night! I don't know who had more fun that night, the sergeants or me and my class mates. We all certainly had wall-to-wall smiles on our faces throughout the sergeants' lecture. I do know who DID NOT have fun that night—the raiding senior class!

Fore!

Strange, and at times, almost unbelievable things happen in police academies. On one of my first nights in residence, I was awakened in the wee hours by a repeated "thwick—swoosh—thunk" sound coming from the hallway outside our dorm. As I peered cautiously out the doorway to investigate these strange sounds, a small white projectile whistled-by my nose and embedded itself with a loud "thunk" in the plasterboard wall at the end of the hallway.

At the other end of the hall was a large common room with a raised ceiling. Turning my attention to that direction, I saw a rather large senior cadet teeing up another golf ball. I ducked back into my room just in time as he drove another brand new Titlest down the hall and into the wall. Needless to say this chap was a little beyond "three-sheets-to-the-wind." However, once he'd woken up a sufficient number of other senior cadets to form a posse; they grappled him to the floor and dragged him away to sleep it off.

The next morning, I again awoke to thumps down the hall. I fully expected more range practice so cautiously peeked out my door. The midnight golfer was pounding the wall at the end of the hall apart with his bare fists. I presumed his objective was to retrieve his golf balls. However, when I politely enquired I found out that such was not the case.

"Golf balls? To heck with the fuckin' golf balls. I'm just making sure the janitor don't rob me blind when he fixes this here wall. Walls get damaged all the time around here so a long time ago a cadet made a deal with the janitor to fix things up for $50 per hole. It don't matter the size of the hole; large or small, it's still $50 per hole."

It was then that I realized that the now almost sober cadet was simply making sure that by the time he finished, the four holes from the previous evening were going to be one big hole, thus saving him $150.00!

Fire in the hole—uh, hair!

Some practical jokes are simply not funny. While at the academy, I joined a group of cadets to take in a pro baseball game at the local stadium. The baseball game itself was uneventful, but the ear-piercing screams of a young lady sitting three rows down from us in the eighth inning sure got our attention.

The lady in question sported a huge afro haircut (yes, it was the 70s and afros were popular back then). Her hairdo was larger than a basketball and presumably held in place by at least one can of hairspray—highly flammable hairspray! So when someone threw a lighted match into her hair—POOF! Smoke, flames, and of course hysterical screams, erupted!

Wyatt Holmes

None of us saw the match fly by, it must have come from above us; but as we watched in horror her hairdo literally started to melt away. While two of her seatmates patted-out the fire with their bare hands, another two—the largest of the four—started climbing in our direction.

"Which one of you fuckers threw the match?" one of them yelled at us, with intended murder and mayhem written all over his face.

"It wasn't us," we replied almost in unison, while turning our heads up the stands behind us. "It must have come from higher up!

"Bullshit! Fess-up you assholes and we'll show you what we do to scumbags like you!"

Why they picked on us is still something of a mystery. There were numerous rows above us filled by kids of all ages also professing no knowledge of the dirty deed. It may have been the short haircuts we sported, as shoulder length hair and afros were the prevailing style back in those days. Perhaps they thought that we were anti-afro skinheads or something. Luckily, one of our self-defence instructors had instructed that the most effective muscle in a police officer's body is his or her tongue. In other words, it's better to talk your way out of a difficult situation than to duke it out, resulting in someone—often the officer—ending up in hospital. Remembering that advice, we continued to profess our innocence in eloquent terms. It was of course impossible to pinpoint the source of the flaming match which started the conflagration so, while shouting various expletives and a few more rather descriptive threats, the "big guys" returned to their seats and the game went on.

It was sure hard to watch the rest of the game as our eyes kept moving back to the poor girl below us with the now bowl-like hairdo surrounding her partially bald scalp.

Simon says...

Even our instructors weren't immune from practical jokes—playing them, that is. As raw cadets, we certainly wouldn't dare play a joke on an instructor.

One day, a crusty old sergeant replaced our regular instructor for a drill class. That's right, "drill" class. Why drill? Well, how do you think police officers look so coordinated in parades and at the inevitable funeral processions of fallen comrades? They learn how to march at the academy—and like elephants, they seldom forget!

Sgt. Brutal was a short chap, but more spit & polished than all the other instructors put together. No one had ever seen him laugh, let alone crack a smile. The news that he was replacing our regular instructor to take us through some drill paces left most of us in abject fear! Well, after marching us around the drill hall for a while, he said, "Now we're going to play 'Simon Says.'"

He refreshed our memories on the childhood game where you have to react to anything the leader premises with "Simon says..." and remain rigidly immobile for any commands issued without the magic lead-in words. Sgt. Brutal started with a few simple commands.

"TROOP, Simon says—RIGHT TURN!"

"TROOP, Simon says—LEFT TURN!"

"TROOP, Simon says—ABOUT TURN!"

He then picked up the pace a little with some commands premised by "Simon says" and some without. As you might guess, he caught out most of the cadets at some point or other during this little exercise; whereupon he would scream at the offenders, "GIVE ME TWENTY!" He was referring, of course, to push-ups. However, after twenty minutes or so there were a few of us left who had yet to fall into his wily traps. Suddenly Sgt. Brutal screamed...

"Simon says—JUMP UP IN THE AIR!"

We all, of course, promptly jumped straight up in the air. Without missing a beat, Sgt. Brutal screamed...

"GIVE ME TWENTY, YOU MORONS!"

With more than a little trepidation, I stuck up my hand and said, "But sergeant, Simon said to jump up in the air and we all jumped up into the air just like... 'Simon said!'" With the one and only smile we ever saw cross his face Sgt. Brutal replied...

"Cadet Holmes; Simon said to jump <u>up</u> in the air. Simon said nothing about coming <u>down</u>! Now, GIVE ME TWENTY YOU MISERABLE RABBLE!"

Three's company—four's a party

Police academies are great places for practical jokes, especially impromptu ones. For most of the 60s and 70s, many police departments hired male sworn officers only. As such, police cadets were frequently on the prowl for casual female companionship. Ironically, many police academies were situated quite close to hospitals, most with training facilities for young nurses. It was therefore not uncommon for cadets to call up the pay phone in the lobby of the nurses' residence and ask if anyone wanted a blind date. Sometimes, the pay phone in the lobby of the cadets' barracks would also ring.

One Saturday morning at breakfast, three cadets decided to try their luck with the lovely ladies down the street. Bill and Bob elected Brian to make the call. Brian had one of those sultry voices that ladies fell for every time. Brian made the call and in no time flat had three nurses lined up for five o'clock that afternoon. Brian, of course, had promised them a night on the town that they'd never forget.

Bill owned the largest car so he was volunteered to drive. Bob rode shotgun in the front with Brian in the rear. On arrival at the nurses' residence, Brian jumped out and jogged up the twenty odd steps to the impressive oaken front door. A few minutes later, out came Brian with the three nurses in tow.

"They were the ugliest nurses we'd ever seen," said Bob, as he told the story over a few beers later that evening; ignoring the fact that he himself wasn't the prettiest looking dude around.

"So what happened'" someone asked anxiously.

"Well, Bill looked at me and I looked at Bill and with a quick nod to each other we were outta there like a cat on a hot tin roof!"

"You could hear Bill's tires squealing three blocks away," laughed Bob. "Talk about black smoke! The smell of burning rubber will hang around the front of that nurses' building 'til the cows come home!"

"But what about Brian?" someone asked.

"Brian who?" Bill and Bob chuckled. "Oh, that Brian—what a dumbass! Well, as he was the one who called them and who brought them out on the front step, we figured he could keep them!" More laughter drowned out further conversation.

At breakfast the next morning we all heard the rest of the story. It appears that ever the chivalrous gentleman, Brian did the honorable thing and took all three ladies out on the town. As he said himself with a wall-to-wall grin, "I promised to take them girls out on the town and that's just what I done. A promise is a promise! Ain't that what they been teaching us here at the police academy?"

Brian didn't say whether the nurses had had a night on the town they'd never forget, but it was pretty clear that he did!

Who wants the rookie?

Fresh out of the academy, I reported to my new department's training sergeant for duty. "Okay Kid," he said, "Let's go find you a partner." He proceeded to lead me into an enormous squad room where 20-30 officers were on the phone, writing-up reports or just standing around sipping coffee. "Gentlemen, I'd like to introduce you to Officer Holmes, the newest member of our department. Now, who wants to show him the ropes?"

As the sergeant issued this invitation, everyone in the room made a mad dash for the exits! Some crammed themselves under desks and others into lockers along the side walls of the squad room. I, of course, was shocked, nonplussed and flabbergasted! After a few seconds, people began to emerge from their hiding places and laughter reigned! I'd known humor and practical jokes during my training days, but I expected more grown-up behaviour from seasoned police officers. As I learned later, this was just a first taste that such was not to be the case! Eventually, one seasoned veteran came out of hiding and offered to take me under his wing.

"I'll take him on Sarg," Officer Matthews said. "I'll show him the ropes and maybe even give him enough of them so he can hang himself!" More laughter followed.

Before I knew it, Matthews had car keys in hand and said, "Okay rookie, let's get our car and get out of here, we've got work to do!"

Now that's what I'd been waiting for—real police work!

Dog!

I jumped into the passenger seat of our tired looking patrol car and asked my seasoned partner—Officer Matthews—when it would be my turn to drive.

"I'll let you know, Kid," he deadpanned. In over 35 years of policing, I never did get an official explanation for the practice, but in most departments, the senior officer usually drives while the junior one tends to the radio, the reports and the inevitable foot pursuits. In fact, the rookie knows when he's made the grade when his partner throws him the keys and then says, "Let's hit the road!"

It was a fairly quiet evening; that is until we got a call of someone drunk & disorderly outside a local tavern. The fellow in question was very large, very inebriated and declared himself ready to take on all comers.

"Come on boys! Shee if you kin took me! You shoulds have brung more than jush the twos of yous! Gonna take a whole squad of yous bastards to take old Frankie alive!"

As mentioned earlier, at the academy we'd been told that a police officer's strongest muscle is his tongue; because an effective officer should be able to talk anyone into or out of just about anything. So within a few minutes, my partner and I had talked our drunken "client" into the back seat of our police car or "PC" (a common abbreviation in police circles prior to the arrival of personal computers). We were now back on the road heading safely for the lock-up. I soon found out that we usually didn't take anyone to court for being drunk & disorderly; we just provided them with a secure place to sleep it off. Most were very appreciative of this type of break and vowed never to return for another night's free accommodation under similar circumstances. Most, of course, broke that promise. Regardless, we reserved court appearances for those few who were truly physically or verbally abusive; in other words, those who really deserved it. As I discovered later, our department also saved a bundle on court-related overtime!

Our latest client suffered in silence for a few minutes, but soon switched gears and started mumbling expletives and veiled threats towards Matthews and me—his uniformed captors.

"Howse I get in here then? he asked, "And howse come I got cuffs on?" Officer Matthews warned him to calm down and enjoy the ride. This resulted in louder threats accentuated by his attempts to smash the police shield using both fists and then both feet. Matthews warned him twice more to "Shut the fuck-up;" all to no avail.

"Dog!" said Matthews, as he suddenly slammed on the brakes.

"What the heck was that all about?" I blurted as I grabbed the dashboard frantically and heard our client's face smack loudly against the Plexiglas guard behind our front seats.

"Mowther of Gawd," slurred our client. "Did ya run over sump'tin yew stewpid suckers?" followed by an impressive list of expletives. A minute or so later, Matthews again abruptly applied the brakes.

"Dog!" he shouted again, a mere millisecond before slamming his foot into the rubber coated pedal. This time I was able to brace for the impact. However, in his inebriated state our client missed the cue and once again slammed into the shield with a resounding Smack!... Squeal!... Expletive!...

"Dog?" I asked, "What dog?"

"That dog!" Matthews replied, slamming on the brakes for a third time.

Smack!... Squeal!... Whimper... then... Silence! Blissful silence all the way back to the lock-up.

"Bet they didn't teach you that at the academy?" my partner chuckled knowingly.

On arrival at the lock-up our client was very polite and cooperative. I was a little surprised to find him completely unharmed from our encounters of the dog kind. It's remarkable what a drunken body can withstand without serious injury.

Over the coming months, I realized that I still had a lot to learn as there were many tricks out there not offered at the academy—some for obvious reasons!

The fine art of surveillance

The first division to which I was assigned believed in giving each rookie a taste of several operational areas before their permanent assignment. So, after gaining some basic street-level experience with Officer Matthews, I eventually moved to a plain clothes unit. One of the tasks in plain clothes was to conduct surveillance on suspected criminal activity. Much of this surveillance occurred "after hours" so to speak.

One night I was with two other officers watching a building where we hoped to check the movements of one of our organized crime suspects. I was sitting in the front passenger seat with Jimmy Argue while Al Richards cat-napped in the back. At some point in the wee hours,

Jimmy told me to switch places with Al. When I opened the car door the interior dome-light came on. In unison, Jimmy and Al screamed at me to close my fucking door!

"Fuck", said Jimmy, "We figured you were smarter than that, rookie. You're supposed to climb over the front seat so the dome-light doesn't go on and blow our cover!"

With a beet-red face, I apologized profusely while trying to get my blood pressure back under control. Then I carefully climbed over the seat and joined Al in the rear. Once I'd made the transition, Al calmly exited by his rear door and jumped in the front. The dome-light, of course, flashed on & off repeatedly like a lighthouse beacon as the back door, and then the front door, opened and closed. I thought both officers were going to choke themselves with laughter! That's when I realized I'd been had—again! Only a few seconds later, however, our target came out of the building and away we went following his car towards the downtown area.

Surveillance is usually conducted with a team of at least four vehicles. The trick is to keep switching places behind and sometimes in front of the target so he or she doesn't see the same vehicle shadowing them all the time. Of course we also tried to keep at least one vehicle between us and the target as additional cover. We called such in between vehicles "dummies." We'd given our targets nicknames and had color-coded many of the main streets in case the objects of our attention were monitoring the authorized police radio bands. Over the police-radio you'd often hear semi-coded conversations like, "Got Mickey Mouse going south on Yellow just past Green with two dummies." Although sworn to uphold all laws, surveillance teams routinely ignored speed limits, stop signs, one-way streets, etc., in order to gain an advantage over a target's movements around the city. Occasionally, other laws were bent or broken. For example, we were parked outside an underground garage one night waiting for a blue Rolls Royce to exit—yeah, crime does pay for some people, but only 'til they get caught! Right on schedule, the Rolls appeared. As it passed our vehicle I noticed that one of its tail-light covers was smashed. The white bulb inside still burned brightly; so brightly in fact that it provided a handy beacon to follow in heavy traffic. I mentioned to my team-mates that I'd never seen a car as fancy as a Rolls Royce with a broken tail-light let alone a broken anything before; to which they just smiled knowingly.

Later that evening, we actually lost the Rolls when another team took the point-position and somehow mistook a Ford with a broken tail-light for the Rolls with a broken tail-light. No one noticed the difference until our unit regained the point-position and Jimmy screamed into the microphone,

"What's going on—that's a fucking Ford ahead of us—where the hell is the Rolls? Are you other guys sleeping on the job, or what?"

"A Ford? Whadda ya mean a Ford? Hey, you're right, that is a Ford—where'd the bloody Rolls get to?"

stuttered the driver of Unit-3, who had just finished passing the target over to us. I guessed I wasn't the only one with a red face that evening.

On another day, we were running surveillance in a hotel near the airport. One of our specialized units was installing electronic monitoring devices or "wiretaps" in our target's hotel room. We'd rented the room next door to the target and one of our technicians was drilling a hole through the wall to hide a microphone behind a painting in the target's room. This was long before the days of tiny self-powered wireless mikes as we see on TV today—our microphone was of the "wired" kind. I was told to stand by the elevator and wait for our target to come back upstairs from the hotel restaurant. I was told very seriously and in no uncertain terms that my job—an important one it seemed—was to stall the target, if necessary, while the technicians finished their job; part of which included entering the target's room undetected to check that their equipment was working.

"How do I stall him?" I asked, realizing that I'd be up against a seasoned criminal who'd likely be suspicious of any obvious delaying tactics.

"Just wing it," my colleagues told me. "Ask him for the time or for directions or something!"

"Ask him for a date!" someone else laughed.

So I stood outside the elevator for about a half hour or so, sweating bullets and hoping that the target didn't come back sooner than expected. Finally, one of our team members came and told me I could stand-down and re-join the group in our room. No one said anything, but from the chuckles and knowing grins around the room I got the distinct impression that everyone but me knew all along that the target was already being shadowed downstairs (duh!) and that my assigned role was actually redundant. I figured later that it had been just one more way to "get the new guy!"

Professor Gunter to the rescue

One day I answered the phone in our squad room and a rather articulate lady told me her house was being inundated with "rays." I thought she was complaining about a propane leak or something, so I told her to call the gas company.

"No," she replied very seriously, "I'm not talking about gas, I'm talking about rays—you know, from ray-guns!" I stood silent for a moment trying to gather my thoughts before my next words were uttered.

"Oh, now I understand, Madam; but this is the police department. I think you should report this matter to one of the local environmental agencies."

"No, no—you don't understand!" she said, "They're the ones shooting the ray-guns at my house!" I quickly asked the lady to hold, telling her I needed to check on the appropriate policy for such a serious matter. Several of the more senior members couldn't help but notice my mix of confusion and pent-up laughter.

"What's up Wyatt?" one of them asked.

I explained the situation and a seasoned officer said, "Let me take it—we get these all the time!" I handed him the phone and he punched the button to release "hold" and spoke to the lady. In a very Germanic accent, I listened to his side of the conversation as he said, "Allo—you have ray problem, ya? Ya! Ya! My name is Professor Gunter. I am a vorld renowned physicist with many years' experience vid such matters. Ya, I am vat you call a physicist—an expert in rays und nuclear stuff, you know? Now, here is vat you must do. Ya, it vill be okay—I promise! Ya, ya—no more rays! I guarantee it! Okay, dees rays cannot penetrate zee valls of your hoose. Zay only come in through zee vindows—ya? Okay, you must take some plastic vrap—ya. Zat is right, zee kind you cover food vid! Ya, you buy dis vrap at zee grocery store—ya! It is easy to fix, ya! You must cover all your vindows with dis plastic vrap. Do not forget zee vindows in your front and back doors! Ya? Guaranteed to vork for you! Ya, ya—of course—no more rays vill enter your home! If protecting the vindows doesn't vork, you'll just have to vrap yourself with the plastic vrap. Yes, only one layer is needed. No, is does not hurt at all. I do it myself all zee time. So, okay now? Ya? No, no—is no problem vat-so-ever; dis is my job you know! Ya—bye, bye!"

We never heard from the lady again!

Money in the bank

On another occasion, the front desk called our squad room to assist a gentleman who had walked in off the street. It being a quiet day, Ernie, another junior officer, joined me for what we thought was an "assistance to general public" call. Sitting near the front desk was an elderly gentleman who could definitely be termed as "a little down on his luck." He was wearing a suit, tie and what may have passed for dress-shoes many years ago, but his current ensemble was soiled and threadbare. Although better dressed, he looked similar to the many other street-people we saw each day panhandling on the sidewalks or sleeping in the alleys downtown. Anyway, mustering up our most professional manner we asked him what his problem was.

The gentleman introduced himself as Arthur Coombes.

"My brother has my bankbook and I can't get any money out of my account," he explained. He went on to tell us that his younger brother had taken his bankbook without permission and may have been making illegal withdrawals from Mr. Coombes' savings account.

"Sounds interesting, Mr. Coombes," said Ernie. "Let's take a walk outside and you can provide us with more details." The suggestion of a walk was partly because it was a beautiful summer's day, but mostly because our new client smelled quite rank and we figured our front lobby would be better off without a lengthy visit from this gent. Out of curiosity and to advance our investigation, I followed up on Ernie's initial comments.

"So, Mr. Coombes, just how much money are we talking about? In your account, I mean?"

"Oh, quite a lot of money," he replied.

"What does 'quite a lot' mean?" I asked.

"Oh, I have at least a million, trillion quadrillion dollars in my account!" he claimed, without a hint of deceit or humor. Ernie swiftly peeled off and hung back a few paces while he tried to compose himself. He then dropped back into step with the elderly gentleman as I took my turn peeling off to stifle a chuckle while pretending to blow my nose into a handkerchief. As luck would have it, we were only a block or two from the closest hospital. On arrival at the emergency room, I proffered my badge to the admitting nurse and explained that we had a possible mental infirmity case for her attention. She looked over my shoulder and sighed loudly…

"Arthur—not again! Are you bothering these nice gentlemen from the police? You know where to sit, Arthur. Now you just stay quiet until I can get someone to take you back to *The Home.*

"A sad case really," she explained, "He used to run a clothing store several blocks away, but after his wife died a few years ago he went downhill quite quickly. He now lives in a rundown retirement home a few blocks from here. They take good care of him, at least when they can him keep him on the premises. He walks away a lot and spends days at a time on the streets looking for his wife. Eventually, someone picks him up and takes him home. We'll look after him, don't you worry!"

Ernie and I walked back to our squad room in silence, both realizing just how lucky we were with our own lot in life.

"George Harrison calling…"

One day we received a request from a department halfway across the country to track down an unlisted phone number in our area. They were investigating a serious crime and needed to know where the individual lived so we could assist them further by starting physical and possibly electronic surveillance. This was many years before "online directory assistance" and "reverse phone number lookup" existed. All the other department had was the name "Frank" and a phone number. It was a rush job and the phone company—which usually cooperated with us on such matters—was closed for the weekend. One bright light suggested we make a "cold call" to the phone number and ask for "Frank." We figured that once we had the guy on the phone we'd chat him up and trick him into revealing his last name and perhaps his address. It's really surprising what one can dig out of people with a little imagination and chutzpah. As most people know, the bad guys run these scams all the time to get banking and other information out of people. There was, of course, nothing illegal in this procedure and as I was the newbie I was assigned to call the mysterious Frank. My call was promptly answered by a woman's voice.

"Is Frank there?" I asked politely.

"Uh," followed by a short pause and then in a trembling voice... "Who's calling please?" Well, you'd think I'd have been better prepared, but I wasn't, so I blurted out the first name which came to mind—my favorite member of The Beatles.

"It's, uh… George... uh, George Harrison. I just need to talk to Frank for a minute." The woman then said…

"Uh... well… Frank's my husband; or I should say he was my husband… he… uh... he died six months ago. I never heard Frank mention your name before; just how did you know my husband?"

By this time I was into major damage-control-mode and stammered something to the effect that I'd worked with Frank several years ago, was in the area, and so thought I'd look him up. When the woman started probing again (which was supposed to me my job), I mumbled some lame excuse and hung up! Thank God we didn't have call-display in those days! I blew part of the investigation that day, but I also learned a valuable lesson—always be prepared!

No wonder Boy Scouts are so smart!

The young entrepreneur

A fellow member of my fraternal order approached me one day to seek some advice about his son.

"You know my boy Bobby. He's only a junior in high school, but the kid has more money than King Midas!" Dave explained. "I don't know where the money comes from, but I'm afraid he's selling drugs to his fellow students. I don't know what to do. If my wife finds out it'll kill her. Lord knows what my mother-in-law would say. Any chance you could have a word with him? I figure he'll open up easier to his old little league coach, even though you're a cop and all."

"I'll see what I can do," I replied.

About a week later, I bumped into Dave in a hardware store. "Did you get a chance to talk to my son," he asked nervously.

"Yes, I did. You were right; he's selling to his fellow students alright. But don't worry, he won't be charged with anything. He's not selling drugs," I said with a big smile on my face, "He's selling condoms!"

I went on to explain that when I approached his son he told me that many of his high school buddies were too embarrassed to buy condoms from the local pharmacy, so he was buying them in bulk and selling them individually for a huge profit.

"Bobby's quite the entrepreneur!" I announced with a chuckle. "Someday your kid's going to be a millionaire!" You know what, today Bobby is indeed a millionaire!

Don't mess with the Judge I

In a large east coast city, the local police had worked tirelessly for many months to put a dent in the local drug trade. They knew the major players; they just couldn't seem to get the break they needed to put one or more of the top drug pushers behind bars. As luck would have it, a routine traffic stop dramatically changed their world. A street-savvy uniformed officer found a handful of joints in the jacket pocket of one of their major targets. Minor stuff in the bigger scheme of things, but a bust is a bust so they decided to take the fellow to court.

"What's going on?" asked the target as the officer snapped on the cuffs. "You're arresting me for a few joints? Heck, you know you're only wasting your time.

Old Judge Harvison will only slap my wrist with a pissant fine. It's gonna cost you more than that just to book me!"

"Don't worry, son," replied the officer. "You may only get a $50 fine, but you've had this coming for a long time and the media attention we'll get for busting your ass will be—priceless!"

The courtroom was full when the fellow made his appearance. Everyone knew the score. Judges, prosecutors, clerks and the local media all knew this chap had been living high-on-the-hog on the wrong side of the law for many years. They figured he was guilty and all waited with bated breath to hear the druggie's side of the story—and to what Judge Harvison would say.

"How does the defendant plead?" asked the judge.

"Guilty as charged your Honor!" answered the cocky druggie with a smirk.

"Plea accepted," announced the judge. "The amount of illicit drugs is hardly significant, so I find myself obliged to follow the normal penalty in such cases by imposing a fine of fifty dollars." Everyone knew the judge's hands were tied by precedent and that only exceptional circumstances would prompt him to raise the bar and drop the axe on the arrogant drug-pusher.

"No problem Your Honor," sniggered the defendant as he swaggered towards the bench while whipping out his wallet. "I've got that in my ass pocket!"

"And six months," said the judge stone-faced as he dropped his gavel with a bang. "You got that in your ass pocket?"

The moral of this story is, of course, "Don't mess with the Judge!"

Don't mess with the Judge II

Some judges are liberal and some are conservative; some are bleeding hearts and some are just plain mean. Occasionally, however, you come across what law enforcement, judicial and correctional workers call a "hanging judge." Judge Hatfield was such a judge.

On one occasion, as he took his legal perch at the front of the court, Judge Hatfield spied someone sitting in the back with his hat on. He promptly stood back up.

"Mister, remove your hat! Yes, I'm talking to you at the back!" His long arm of the law pointed ominously towards the rear of the courtroom. "I don't allow the wearing of hats in my courtroom, No Sir!" he bellowed.

On another occasion, someone walked in on a trial in progress. He wasn't wearing a hat, but he wasn't wearing a shirt either. Judge Hatfield stopped the defence attorney's questioning in mid-stride and shouted, "Hey, you! Yes, you there without the shirt! Get the heck out of my court before I find you in contempt! Bailiff, remove that man from my sight! No one enters my courtroom without proper attire; No Sir – No One!"

One afternoon, just before adjourning for the day, the bailiff called the next case to the bar.

"John Grant! Please come forward." No one budged.

"Is John Grant in the court today?" Still no movement and with all eyes on the judge, silence reigned.

"For the third time, would Mister John Grant please step forward?"

"What's the charge?" asked Judge Hatfield.

"Drunk & disorderly, Your Honor," answered the bailiff.

"Was he served notice of the time and date for his appearance?" asked the judge.

"It says here that he was, Your Honor. Yes, Sir, he was definitely served, Your Honor."

"Does anyone know where John Grant is?" continued the judge, now directing his voice to the assembly as he scanned all present with a haughty frown.

Just then, a woman at the back of the room stood up. In a quavering voice she said that she'd seen Mr. Grant in court after lunch, but he'd left about an hour ago mumbling something about quenching his thirst.

"Officer Holmes," said Judge Hatfield quietly, turning his attention to myself. "There are three bars within walking distance of this courtroom and I suspect our friend is in one of them. Would you be so kind as to run along and—FIND HIM!"

"Yes Sir, Your Honor, Sir," I managed to stammer as I hit the door at a run.

As it happened, I didn't have to find John Grant. Without any outside assistance, Grant managed to quench his thirst and find his way back to the courthouse all by himself. I missed all the fun, as I was still searching bars; but from all accounts when Grant staggered back into the courtroom he was wearing a ball cap and no shirt. Before he reached an available seat, he belched once and fell flat on his face.

"Mister Grant, I presume?" sneered Judge Hatfield, as he raised a hand to interrupt the ongoing proceedings.

"Yesh, your judge-sheep," replied John Grant, as he crawled up the side of the closest bench. "Thash's me alright! John Auguthstus Grant – in the ful-lesssh!"

"Mister Grant," smiled Judge Hatfield—eyes burning brightly and hardly breaking stride, "I accept your plea of guilty on the count of being drunk & disorderly on the fifth of this month. I also accept your plea of guilty on a second count of being drunk & disorderly today, here in my courtroom! I also find you in contempt of this court for having the temerity to come in here wearing a hat and without a shirt to boot! On all counts I sentence you to a fifty-dollar fine and three days in jail. Officers, remove this man from my sight! Bailiff, next case please!"

Remember folks… "Don't mess with the Judge!"

Shoot, reload, and shoot again!

As I gained experience, I found myself being sought out by my younger colleagues for advice on a variety of topics. At one point I moved to a rural environment and found the change of pace quite refreshing. We still picked up drunks and impaired drivers, still investigated thefts and house break-ins, and still spent most of our time doing routine patrols. But rural policing does have its moments.

It was about three o'clock one morning when I got a call from our latest rookie on patrol. He apologized for waking me and then asked for my assistance or at least for my advice.

"I'm at a traffic accident on a dirt road out in the back forty," Morris said. "A pick-up truck has hit a horse and the bloody thing is injured badly and in pain. It's lying in a muddy ditch and the farmer wants me to put-it-down. Am I allowed to do that?" he queried.

"Does this farmer own the horse?" I asked.

After a short pause and some background whispering he replied, "Yes! It's his horse and he just wants me to put it out of its misery."

"Okay, Morris, so long as it's his horse, you can put it down for him. Do you have a rifle with you?"

"Nope, just my revolver," he replied, referring to his officially issued sidearm.

Now a horse is a fairly large animal, one that would usually be put-down by a high calibre weapon. Our issue sidearm at the time was a Smith & Wesson .38 Special six-shot revolver—a far cry from the firepower carried by most modern police officers. The venerable .38 was not the most powerful firearm, but it was much better than the standard .22 calibre stuff most farmers carried to deal with rabbits, ground hogs and the like. It just so happened that my girlfriend's father was a butcher. Nick bought & sold local meat and I'd helped him dispatch a few animals from time to time. As such, I felt fairly comfortable giving some "put-down" advice to our rookie.

"Okay, your service revolver will do fine. Just listen carefully. A horse has a pretty thick skull, but they have a weak spot in their forehead right between their eyes. If you hit that spot with your .38 you should put the beast down without any problem."

"Okay, thanks a lot, Wyatt. Go back to sleep, I've got this under control."

The next morning a squad-room full of officers changing shifts heard the full story from the rookie. It seems as soon as he lined up his sights on the horse's forehead he faced a chorus of farmers all telling him to shoot the animal in the neck. "But there's a weak spot right there!" he tried to explain to them—all to no avail.

"A horse is just like a deer or an elk," said one wizened old farmer with authority. "Everyone knows you shoots them animals in the neck!"

"Yeah, he's right son," offered another tiller of the soil. "In the neck! If he don't die from the shot, he'll bleed-out in a couple of minutes or so." So, surrounded by insistent farmers and with my advice rapidly fading from his mind, Morris explained how he moved to one side and shot the horse in the neck.

The next thing Morris knew he was flat on his back in the muddy ditch with the horse rearing up above him, hooves a-flailing away wildly!

"I emptied my gun into him and reloaded as fast as I could," our rookie explained seriously. "I gave him another six rounds and he finally fell to the ground."

"Was he dead?" someone asked between chuckles.

"Uh, not exactly," came the reply. "But I got more bullets out of my patrol car and gave him the *coup de grace!*" he said with a flourish.

"Where'd you hit him for the *coup de grace?*" I asked with a knowing smile.

"Uh, right between the eyes!" said Morris with a sheepish grin. "They have a weak spot there you know!"

Huff & Puff & Blow!

One time I pulled over a suspected DUI (driver under the influence). I brought the driver in to the office for a breathalyser test. He'd already failed the standard roadside tests of breathing in my face, trying to walk a straight line and touch his finger to his nose—this was long before the arrival of modern handheld electronic roadside testing devices. At the office, I handed my client over to the on-duty breathalyser operator. I was still pretty junior and not yet qualified to administer breathalyser tests, but I knew a fair bit about the machines by watching other officers administer the tests. After prepping the machine, the operator clipped a mouthpiece to the end of a long tube and told my client to blow as hard as he could for as long as he could.

"It's just like blowing up a balloon for your kid's birthday party," he offered. "Take a deep breath and then give it your all into this here mouthpiece!" The deepest recesses of your lungs hold the highest concentration of alcoholic fumes so deep breaths were what we needed for an accurate reading. I thought the fellow blew pretty hard, but the operator wasn't satisfied.

"You're not blowing hard enough, buddy! he said, pointing to the machine. "I need a proper sample for this thing to work properly. When you blow hard enough you'll know it, 'cause this little light here will flash green." So the fellow tried again—same result. After a couple more unsatisfactory tries, the operator's voice took on a more ominous tone.

"Listen fellow, if you don't give me a proper sample I'll have to cite you for refusing to blow! That charge carries the same penalty as driving under the influence so let's try again, okay?"

My client was pretty red in the face by this time and in my opinion just about at the point of fainting. I figured he'd given it his all so took a closer look at the machine he was blowing into. It was then I noticed that a small switch on the side of the machine had not been turned on. I quickly nudged the operator and nodded towards the switch.

While developing a rosy-flushed face, the operator deftly flicked the switch as my client jumped into full and final blow-mode. He deflated in an instant and the operator exclaimed, "There, I told you you'd get it eventually!"

Honeymoon or not, you're it!

Lengthy summer vacations were reserved for officers with families; so when I married it was with no surprise that I readily accepted my boss's offer of a mere seven-day honeymoon. Once back in town, my bride and I organized our new apartment, switched off the lights and settled in for a good night's sleep. Then the phone rang. It was 3:12 a.m. It was the regional 911 dispatcher.

"Officer Holmes," she said with tension in her voice," There's been a bad accident about ten miles out of town. I need you to attend the scene and report back a.s.a.p." I quickly explained that I wasn't on duty or even on-call, and indeed that I was still on my honeymoon.

"I'm sorry for the inconvenience, Holmes; but everyone else is already occupied elsewhere. You're the only one I've been able to reach and I need you at that accident scene—right now!" We were a largely rural agency with limited resources. The operator told me she'd even tried calling the Chief. The Chief lived adjacent to the office so he could field some of the smaller complaints during the off hours when no one was on duty. If he too was incommunicado, I realized I was left with no choice but to kit-up and get on the road!

The accident had been reported as an overturned eighteen-wheeler with serious injuries—the dispatcher said I'd better hurry! So, slipping quickly into uniform and offering an even quicker goodbye kiss to my new bride, off I went. As I squealed into the police parking lot to pick up a police car, I noticed lights on inside—strange at that time of night; especially if all other officers were occupied elsewhere. When I tried the front door it was unlocked— the plot thickened. Inside, I was greeted by the Chief and a couple of other officers. All were laughing heartily and I realized that I'd been had once again.

My buddies of course dragged me back into the boss's kitchen to join them for a healthy glass of rum & coke (hardly their first I might add), before letting me return home. Suitably fortified, I decided to get a bit of payback on the 911 dispatcher who'd been in on the trick. Everyone else also thought this a great idea! So, we dialled up the emergency number.

"911, do you require police, fire or ambulance?" the operator asked calmly, coolly and very professionally.

"It's me, Officer Holmes," I shouted while feigning shortness of breath; "I've got bodies all over the road here and need back-up a.s.a.p. I've got two confirmed dead and will need at least two ambulances for the injured. A couple are really bad and one of the cars is on fire, so you'd best call out the fire department too! Please hurry— it's a real mess out here!" Silence prevailed at the other end of the line.

"Uh, Officer Holmes" asked the operator, "Are you at the accident scene?"

"Yes, of course. Please hurry, I need help out here!

"Uh, well, just what phone are you calling from?" asked the operator; her confusion magnified by knowledge that the location to which she'd sent me was a little isolated with absolutely no houses, farms or payphones along the way.

"From a phone-booth in the back of the overturned semi-trailer you sent me to! Where else do you think I'd be calling from?" I gasped, trying unsuccessfully to stifle my laughter.

"Okay, okay, very funny!" she finally laughed back at me, now hearing laughter from my buddies also. "You got me! Tell those assholes this is the last time I help them with a practical joke at three in the morning! Now go back to bed and enjoy the rest of your honeymoon!"

So I did – and I did!

Don't mess with the Judge III

As already mentioned, during my thirty-five years on the job I was able to enjoy the challenges of policing a rural community for several years. We were a long way from nowhere and miles from the closest traffic light, let alone any type of four-lane highway. Our office space was limited. It consisted of one open office, one closed office, one interview room, one restroom, one storage cupboard, and one holding cell. Our town didn't have a regular courthouse and the area's judicial needs were serviced by a circuit judge who visited our somewhat isolated community twice a month. We were so far off the beaten track that the duties of bailiff fell to whichever officer was on duty when the travelling judge came to town.

One cold fall day I ended up as bailiff in front of Judge Scott. Judge Scott wasn't what you'd call a hanging judge, but he was certainly well known for his by-the-book attitude and lack of humor. We'd already recessed for lunch and were back in the old schoolhouse which served as both community hall and bi-monthly courtroom. The judge and I were on the home stretch of hearing cases when I called Ernest Pritchard to the docket.

"Ernest Pritchard, please come forward!" I intoned in a serious voice. No one moved in the packed room. Yes, despite our isolation, the room was packed. It was always packed on court days; not full of criminals and other miscreants, but full of anxious spectators because court sessions provided one of the few forms of entertainment in the area. I called for Ernest Pritchard for a second and then a third time to no avail. Ernest was not in the courtroom on that particular afternoon.

"Your Honor," I said, turning officiously to Judge Scott, "It would appear Mister Pritchard is not around today. Perhaps the court might consider issuing an arrest warrant so we can make sure he's here for the next time you visit?"

"Do you know where Mister Pritchard is, Officer Holmes? Judge Scott asked politely.

"No, Your Honor, but I'll make sure he's here next time if you'd kindly issue a warrant."

"Are you telling me you have absolutely no idea where he is? asked the judge again with a smile (although at the time I thought it might have been gas).

"Uh… no, Your Honor," I replied nervously.

"Well, perhaps this would be a good time for a short recess."

"Yes, Your Honor. All rise! This court stands adjourned for…"

"Five minutes," offered the judge.

"For five minutes!" I announced.

"Officer Holmes," smiled the judge, "Perhaps you'd care to join me in my chambers?"

I followed Judge Scott into an adjacent storage room which held a small desk and two chairs. Hardly a judge's "chambers" but when that's all you've got—well, it's all you've got.

"Have a seat, Officer Holmes," said Judge Scott as he settled into the more comfortable of the two chairs—the one with a faded felt seat and both armrests still intact. "You really don't know where Ernest Pritchard is, do you?" he asked, now openly smiling like the proverbial Cheshire cat.

"No Your Honor I don't; but I have a funny feeling that I should know where he is."

"Yes... yes you should," continued the judge. "You might remember that he came up before me two weeks ago and I remanded him to the regional lock-up for reappearance today. I was under the impression that you were going to go get him this morning for us."

"Oh shit!" I exclaimed suddenly, as my memory flooded back with a vengeance. "Uh... I apologize, Your

Honor. Uh, I guess I forgot to go get him yesterday. I'm sorry for forgetting and also sorry for saying "shit" and, oops, I said it again; well—I guess I'm just plain sorry, very sorry, Your Honor - SIR!" Truth be told, I was more terrified than sorry. A long silence seemed to suck up most of the air in the little room as the judge twirled his thumbs with a mischievous twinkle in his eyes.

"Oh well, everyone makes mistakes," said Judge Scott suddenly. "What do you say I remand Mr. Pritchard for another two weeks? We both know he's one of our regulars. When he returns I'm sure he'll plead guilty as usual and then I'll sentence him to time served. Does that work for you, officer?"

"Absolutely, Your Honor!"

"Oh, one last thing, Officer Holmes."

"Yes, Your Honor?"

"Don't forget Mister Pritchard next time!"

Don't hang me, Your Honor!

While still quite junior in service, I accepted a transfer to another rural sector of our department. On my first night-patrol, the dispatcher reported a distraught woman on the line fearful that her elderly brother was about to commit suicide. My new partner, Jake, and I raced to the scene.

On arrival, a near hysterical lady met us in the driveway of an old farmhouse. Pointing to an outhouse out back, she explained that her elderly and very booze-soaked brother was holed-up inside the exterior privy. He was threatening to end his life. Although the area was new to me, Jake had worked this particular countryside for several years and was familiar with this old fellow. He told the woman to coax her brother out of the outhouse and promised that we'd do the rest.

"Come back to the house, Charles," she pleaded. "It's warmer there and I'll make you some tea."

"No! You've called the police and they'll take me away again!"

"Don't be silly. I'm your sister, why would I call the police? Come out and I'll make you some soup; you know how you love my homemade pea soup."

"No. You'll call the police because you just said you would a few minutes ago!"

"Oh for heaven's sake, Charles, I was only joking. The kettle's boiling and the tea is almost ready. Come on out now. You'll catch your death if you stay out here much longer!"

This went on for quite some time while Jake and I crept up on the outhouse. Our legs were starting to stiffen up from crouching in the shadows when Charles finally stumbled out from his hiding place, probably hoping to make a run for it.

"Gotcha," said Jake triumphantly as he grabbed Charles' arm. After a quick frisking, we put him in handcuffs and settled him into the back of our police cruiser.

"Oh, I knew the police were here!" lamented Charles. "Sister, they'll hang me for sure this time! I'm a goner now! Oh, Lord. What have I done?"

"Settle down, Charles," said Jake with a smile to the sister. "No one's gonna hurt you; we'll just get you to a warm holding cell where you can sleep it off again. It's breakfast on the county again for you Charles." However, as soon as we drove off in the direction of our rural detachment, my partner's tone changed.

"Charles, Charles, Charles," Jake tisked-tisked solemnly. "What are we supposed to do with you now?"

"No! No! Please don't hang me!" replied Charles, "I'll be good. I'll never drink again, I promise!"

"Well, you know what Sheriff Booker told you the last time we picked you up for being drunk & disorderly. He said one more time and he'd have to hang you from the neck 'til you were dead—Dead—DEAD! Now start saying your prayers Charlie-boy. You've still got a few minutes coming to you, but only because I personally don't yet have my hanging license. Otherwise I'd a strung you up right outside that there shitter back on your sister's farm. But only Sheriff Booker has the authority to hang people around here." With a loud moan, Charles curled up on the backseat of our patrol car and whimpered all the way back to the office.

"What the heck are you talking about," I whispered to Jake, quite confident in my own knowledge of the law. "Hanging license? What the hell are you talking about? What hanging license?"

"Just havin' a little fun," Jake chuckled.

Knowing full well that John Booker monitored the police radio band after hours, Jake picked up the mike to call the good sheriff at home. After a brief conversation, Sheriff Booker agreed to drive in and meet us at the office. I was still very much in the dark about what was going on.

On our arrival, Sheriff Booker's car was parked in the driveway; however, when we carried Charles into the building there was no sight of our fearless leader. I sat Charles down and started filling out the proper arrest form, while Jake strolled down the hall to the sheriff's private office. A couple of minutes later, Jake strode quickly by us towards the holding cell. He seemed to be trying—unsuccessfully—to stifle a rather unprofessional giggle. The next thing I knew, Sheriff Booker came into the room. He was a tall and imposing man from the get-go. However, on the night in question, he'd donned a fluorescent raincoat, added a reflective vest and riot helmet, and had his hands clad in large yellow heavy rubber gloves (the ones we used to carry decomposing bodies). Charles staggered to his feet as Sherriff Booker intoned dramatically…

"Charles Muldoon Matheson the Third; you have been found drunk and disorderly for the umpteenth and final time! You were warned Mister Matheson. You were warned repeatedly what the consequences of continued drinking of Satan's liquor would bring down upon your head! Now it is time to accept your punishment like a man and go to meet your maker!"

Charles almost fainted dead away right then and there! Heck, I damned near fainted myself! I needed Charles to sign the arrest form acknowledging my seizure of his personal effects, but he was shaking so violently that it was impossible for him to hold a pen, let alone sign his name.

"How does the prisoner plead?" asked Sheriff Booker slowly. Charles blanched as his knees buckled.

"Guilty!" I offered, trying to be helpful and perhaps starting to get with the spirit of the evening. After all, poor old Charles was obviously much too petrified to speak for himself.

"The penalty is death!" continued the sheriff. "By the power invested in me by our sacred Constitution, I hereby sentence you to be hanged by the neck until you are dead—Dead—DEAD!" The sheriff then reached down and, grabbing hold of one of Charles' arms with his rubber gloves, escorted our now very distraught prisoner to the holding cell.

I figured we'd all had our fun and that Jake and the sheriff would now bed Charles down for the night—how wrong could I have been!

As I finished up the paperwork, I could hear Sheriff Booker and Jake talking together in the holding cell. Their voices sounded very officious, until all of a sudden I heard a loud bang followed by maniacal shrieks. Then, after hearing the cell door slam shut, I saw Chief Booker and Jake come running through the squad room and down the hall to the sheriff's office. Both were white as sheets and giggling hysterically. I swear at least Jake passed some nervous gas as he rounded the desk near the hallway. Still not sure what was going on, I ran to the holding cell to check on Charles Muldoon Matheson III. Mr. Matheson was fast asleep curled up in one corner of the cell's bunk. He had gathered the blanket up under his chin just like a toddler and looked very peaceful. I noticed that in their rush the boys hadn't even closed the cell door. However, at least they'd removed the prisoner's belt; standard procedure and one of the last things one does before securing someone for the night. As I locked the cell door I picked up the belt off of the floor—now strangely in two pieces—to add to Charles' personal effects. I then strolled down the hall to find out what all the fuss was about.

It seems the good sheriff kept a bottle of sipping whisky in one of his desk drawers. I don't know how full it was before I entered his office, but by the time I spied it, it was almost empty. When I walked in, Jake was sucking back another belt before handing the bottle back to Sheriff Booker.

"What the heck's going on, Boss?" I asked innocently.

In an erratic manner, Jake explained that they'd had problems with Charles Muldoon Matheson for many years and had decided some time ago to try and convince him to quit drinking once and for all. Nothing else had worked, so they'd decided to try and scare him into sobriety. While Sheriff Booker was playing out the role of judge, jury and executioner in the squad room, Jake had looped a thin piece of rope over the light fixture just outside the cell. When escorted into the holding area, the sheriff had fashioned a simple noose and put it around poor Charles' neck. Then, with one hand raised in a solemn gesture, the sheriff had grabbed Charles by his belt and raised him up to complete the charade. It was at that moment that Charles' belt snapped! You can imagine how the rest unfolded: the maniacal shrieks; the rendered belt falling to the floor; Booker and Jake putting Charles gently to bed; both forgetting to close the cell door; and finally, the white faced scamper to find solace in a similar bottle which had led Charles down his own sorry path. Both

Sherriff Booker and Jake wasted no time in swearing me to secrecy as to the events of that hairy evening.

Charles Muldoon Matheson III died a few years later. He died of accidental causes; that is if drowning in a puddle of dirty water while hammered out of one's skull can be considered accidental. By that time, I'd moved on and was back working in the city. However, one of my investigations led me back to Sheriff Booker's isolated rural area. Jake too had moved on, but the good sheriff was still there. As we sat in the squad room chatting, I mentioned the name of Charles Muldoon Matheson—and suddenly the lights dimmed, albeit briefly.

"Whoa there fella!" said the sheriff with a shiver. "We don't mention that name around here anymore, Son. After that dude passed, the lights dimmed each and every time someone mentioned his name, so we just don't mention it no more! No Sir-ee! We just decided to leave old what's his name to rest in peace—and I suggest you do likewise!"

Good for goose & gander

One of the more pleasurable tasks of police work is traffic law enforcement. You get to meet a wide variety of citizens while conducting routine checks or handing out tickets to keep the coffers of local governments topped-up. One favourite tool of traffic law enforcement is radar.

Although developed independently by various nations in the late 1800s and the early part of the 20th century, British researchers are largely credited with creating the first effective radar units. These were used to protect England from German air attacks during World War II. However, the units we used to check the speed of vehicles in the 70s and 80s were a far cry from the cumbersome units in use in the 40s. They were also a far cry from the laser guns used in more modern times. Either way, radar is very effective. Heck, spell "radar" backwards and it still spells "radar," so that's how the police get you both coming and going!

The antennae of our old units were hung outside a patrol car's window; similar to the speakers we used to hang inside our cars when at the local drive-in theatre. We then calibrated these black boxes using a tuning fork. Once set up, we'd watch the traffic and the needle on the unit's dial to match-up a vehicle and its speed. Our units were not foolproof, however, as a flight of birds or even branches blowing in a gust of wind might influence the magic dial. Proper training and good note taking were amongst the keys to successful convictions.

One beautiful fall afternoon Kevin and I were running a radar trap on a straightaway just around a curve and over a slight rise in the highway. That's right—a "radar trap." By the time a speeding vehicle made the turn and slipped over the little knoll, our radar unit had already captured its speed. We'd issued several tickets already when a small black car whipped into the invisible beam and snapped the needle to 88 mph on our radar's dial.

"Got him," said Kevin. "Eighty-eight in a fifty-five zone. 'Book 'im, Danno!'" Kevin knew my name wasn't Danno, but after many weeks of following the popular "Hawaii Five-O" television series, we both had Steve McGarrett's signature sign-off down pat! I flagged down the car and walked up to the driver's window. Before I got there, a young fellow jumped out.

"What's the matter?" he asked cockily. "Slow day, officer?"

"No, actually pretty fast—at least for you. We just clocked you at 88 in a 55 mile-per-hour zone. May I see your driver's license and registration, please?"

At first the young fellow played dumb, like he hadn't seen the posted speed limit. When I told him 88 mph was well beyond any posted speed within a hundred, maybe a thousand miles around, he switched into his "poor student" act. He claimed to be attending law school with the intent of one day being a police officer just like me. I'd heard it all before, of course. When he finally realized that despite his pleas for mercy he was getting a ticket for speeding anyway, he got pretty mouthy. He started asking all sorts of questions about our experience, the quality of our radar machine and the like. "Save it for the judge." I told him as I handed him his ticket.

"Damn right I will. I know my rights. I'm going to fight this all the way to the Supreme Court!" he squealed, as he climbed back into his car and drove off down the highway.

"It takes all types," offered Kevin, with a frown. "I think we'd better dot all the "I's" and cross all the "T's" on this one. It sounds like he might be anxious for his day in court."

It has been said that the wheels of justice grind along slowly. True to fashion, it was several months later when we met up with our young student again; this time across a crowded courtroom. He'd already entered a plea of not guilty some weeks earlier.

The prosecuting attorney introduced the case at hand and, after establishing our *bona fides*, questioned Kevin and I on our procedures on the day we handed the young fellow his speeding ticket. At one point I asked if I could refer to my police notebook.

"Objection, Your Honor!" said the student, jumping to his feet. "I'd like to know just when the officer's notes were made!"

"If it pleases the court," continued the prosecutor, "Officer Holmes, could you tell us when you jotted down your notes on this case?"

"They were scribbled in draft at the scene of the offence a few minutes after the defendant left the scene," I replied, "and finished up in greater detail back at my office about an hour or so later."

"Your Honor," the student railed, "Jurisprudence is clear that only notes made at the time and place of an offence are admissible at trial. I move that the officer be only allowed to reference his draft notes taken at the scene."

"You've made a good point there, young fellow," said the judge, with a smile. "Officer, you may refer to your notes; but only those made immediately following your interaction with the accused. You may not refer to any notes made later at your office." The young student thanked the judge and threw me an evil grin.

When his turn came, the young student questioned Kevin and me. One area the defendant harped on was the distance his car had been from our vehicle when captured by our radar unit. I wasn't able to directly reference my notes on this as I'd jotted down the exact distance once back in the office, but I was able to state "from memory" that the distance in question was approximately 225 yards. Kevin's memory mirrored my own in this respect, which was hardly surprising as we'd already consulted our notes the day before the trial as part of standard procedure in preparation for trial. Asking the judge for permission to refer to our notes was simply part of the standard theatrics of trial proceedings. Once the student finished questioning us, the judge invited him to introduce the first witness in his defence.

"I only have one witness, Your Honor—myself!" he declared proudly. Someone once said that a person who defends himself has a fool for a lawyer. Well, our young friend was about to prove the truth of that somewhat tired adage.

Once sworn in, the student proceeded to explain how he'd been stopped by Kevin and me. His evidence was basically the same as ours, except when it came to how far away his car had been when captured by our radar unit. While we'd testified to a distance of 225 yards, the defendant stated that he'd measured the distance as being over 400 yards. As he did so, he asked the judge for permission to introduce defence exhibit #1, a scale drawing which reproduced the highway scene we'd shared so many months before. Before the judge could even answer, the defendant started mounting his exhibit on a portable easel for all to behold. We could see that considerable work had been put into sketching the stretch of road in question. The angle of the curve had been calculated and even the slight rise in the highway had been graded. Our seasoned prosecutor rose to his feet.

"If it pleases the Court," he enquired, "Might the defendant advise when and where this exhibit was prepared and specifically, the exact time and date when the distances used for this artwork were measured and recorded?"

The judge smiled.

"Yes, it does please the court," he said. "Could the defendant please answer the question? Exactly when were the measurements taken?" The defendant paled slightly.

"Uh, well Your Honor," he stammered shakily, "I personally took these measurements and spent considerable time preparing my exhibit."

"Yes, I understand all that," replied the judge, "But when did you do all of this fine work?"

"Uh, well—last weekend, Your Honor," mumbled the student, his face now a pasty shade of grey.

"If it pleases the Court…" started the prosecutor; only to be cut short by the judge with a wave of his hand, as if to invite him to sit back down and enjoy the show.

"As you yourself have already argued;" explained the judge to the student, "Only notes made at the time and place of the offence may be relied upon by the court. As the saying goes, 'What's sauce for the goose is sauce for the gander.' As such, I find myself obliged to refuse the admission of your very nice drawing into evidence. Do you have any further evidence to present young man?"

"No Your Honor," whispered the deflated student, as he slouched down in his chair.

"Then I find for the prosecution and sentence the defendant to pay the standard fine. I think we've all learned some valuable lessons today. Court is adjourned!"

Frontier lie-detector

Lie-detector machines, or "polygraphs," as they are more commonly known, are just one of the many specialized tools police officers use in their pursuit of justice. Polygraphs measure several (poly) physical responses such as heart rate, blood pressure, breathing rate and perspiration; and then record the responses on a moving strip of paper (graph). Interpreted by a highly trained examiner, such graphs can indicate whether a person is being truthful or not. However, while a great tool, polygraphs are not infallible.

Polygraphs *indicate*, they do not *confirm*. That's why they are never entered into evidence in court. However, polygraph examiners are not just trained in the *use* of their machines; they are also highly trained in *interview and interrogation techniques.* While all police officers learn how to question suspects; polygraph examiners raise such probing to a whole new level.

The examiner starts by hooking up the suspect person or "candidate" to the polygraph machine. During this process, the examiner explains to the candidate how the machine works; that is, what it measures and how. The examiner then runs the candidate through a few sample questions and instructs the candidate to alternate his or her responses with either the truth or a lie.

"Okay, Mister Ryan Jones. Is your name really Ryan Jones?

"Yes it is."

"Just yes or no answers, please."

"Yes.

"That's good. Now please answer with a lie. Is your name really Ryan Jones?"

"No."

"Very good; now truthfully, please—do you live at 123 Main Street?"

"Yes."

"And now with a lie—do you live at 123 Main Street?"

"No."

"Very good, thank you!"

The examiner then proceeds to show the candidate the graph and how the readings differed when he told the truth or told a lie. This preamble is to convince the candidate that the machine actually works and believe you me, the technique works very well!

The examiner then follows up with questions more pertinent to the investigation at hand. The examiner will ask the same questions several different ways in an attempt to confirm facts or to trip-up the candidate. Although polygraphs can be beaten, the vast majority of candidates end up either being exonerated or confessing to their crime. Once they confess, their confession is duly recorded and THAT is what's used in a court of law.

One of my rural postings was way out in the boonies and a long way from a polygraph machine—let alone a skilled examiner. I was on night patrol with a veteran officer when we received a call of a break, enter and theft at a local liquor store. When we arrived on the scene, the liquor store owner held a young fellow by the scruff of his neck.

"I seen this little bastard loitering around out back, right after I heard the glass break," the owner explained. He says he had nothing to do with it, but as far as I'm concerned he's as guilty as sin!"

"Well now," said my partner, "Let's check this out on the polygraph machine!" *Polygraph machine?* I thought. *What the heck is he talking about, we ain't got no polygraph machine with us?*

"Jump in the back of our car young fella," said Manny. "Hand me the polygraph would you, Wyatt?" gesturing towards the microphone of our police radio. Manny then proceeded to wrap the cord of the microphone around the arm of our young suspect, while keeping the actual mike hidden in his hand out of sight.

"Now young fella," Manny intoned. "You see the box on the dash there, pointing to the police radio. If you tell the truth the green light will light up. However, if you lie, no light will go on. So, truth—light; lie—darkness! You got it?"

"Uh… yes Sir, I got it. But I had nothing to do with the broken glass—I promise!"

"Whoa back, young fella. Just answer my questions, okay?"

"Okay."

Manny then proceeded to explain how the "polygraph" worked to our unsuspecting "candidate." He asked the boy's name, address, age, etc., and told him when to tell the truth and when to lie. Whenever Manny knew the kid told the truth, he'd key the mike so that the light on the dash would blink "on."

"Okay, kid. Now for the tough part. Did Mister Palmer catch you out behind his store tonight?"

"Yes, he did; but I…"

"Just yes or no—just like we practised, okay?"

"Yes." The light on the dash blinked green!

"Did Mister Palmer accuse you of breaking into his liquor store?"

"Yes!" The light once again blinked green!

"Did you indeed break into his liquor store?"

"No!" The light on the dash remained dark, although the kid's eyes were glued to it like his life depended upon it.

"I ask you again, did you break into his liquor store tonight?"

"No" The light stayed dark.

"Are you sure?"

"Well..." The light on the dash flickered for a moment—then died. The kid's eyes were now the side of saucers and he began to tremble.

"Ah ha!" said Manny triumphantly. "Now we're getting somewhere!"

"DID YOU BREAK INTO THE DAMN LIQUOR STORE—YES OR NO?"

"YES! YES! I did it! I'm sorry! Me and the boys just wanted a few beers." The light on the dash blinked wildly as Manny quickly wrapped up the questioning.

"You and the boys? What boys? And don't lie to me son, you're in deep enough shit already—the truth now!"

Oh how the canary sang! And that's how we ended up arresting not just one, but five young fellows for break, enter and theft that fine evening!

Stop or I'll shoot!

Kids will be kids and odd push & shove matches are all part of growing up. However, no one likes a bully. Bullies exist, of course, in all walks of life. Some are physical bullies and some are psychological bullies. Some get over it as they mature and some don't. As fate would have it, some bullies eventually get their just desserts.

One day dispatch called with a complaint of a kid being beat up on by a couple of older boys. At the scene my partner, Ronnie, and I met Billy and his parents. Billy—ten years old and all of eighty pounds soaking wet—said he'd been attacked by Frankie and Lewis. My partner and I were familiar with both boys. Frankie was 15 and had already seen the inside of a police car many times. Lewis was 17 and just a few months shy of graduating from the back seat of a police car to the inside of a jail cell. Once Lewis hit 18 he'd be subject to the adult courts. Both Ronnie and I agreed that barring a miracle, both boys were destined to spend the rest of their days getting into or out of one scrape or the other.

After taking Billy's statement and snapping some photographs of his scratches and bruises, we set out to find the two bullies. It didn't take long.

"There they are," pointed Ronnie. "Let's get ahead of them. We can park on Third Street and surprise them when they come out near the schoolyard." However, as luck would have it, the two boys were a little fleeter of foot than we expected and they saw us pull up to the curb on Third.

"Can we have a word or two fellows?" said Ronnie as we climbed out of our cruiser. Of course, that was all the invitation they needed to hightail it across the schoolyard and disappear towards downtown. "Let's go," shouted Ronnie. "I'll get Lewis—you take Frankie!" I realized that my younger partner was doing me a favour as Frankie was short and chubby while Lewis was quite athletic. So off we went—the two bullies split up just past the school. Before I knew it we'd covered several hundred yards and I was starting to huff & puff big time. Frankie was also slowing down, but then without warning he started to scale a ten foot high chain link fence like a regular chimpanzee. He was almost at the top when I shouted out to him.

"Stop or I'll shoot!" My service pistol was, of course, still secure in its holster; but I had no intention of following Frankie up the fence so figured I'd try to slow him down with a little verbal encouragement. It worked. Frankie fell back to the ground and I slipped the cuffs on him as I read him his rights. We walked back to the cruiser and, after a very quick frisking; I secured Frankie in the backseat. A few minutes later, Ronnie came running up empty handed.

"I lost him on Sixth Street," he explained in a winded voice, "You look like you've had a rest Wyatt, why don't you take a walk down that way and I'll take Frankie back to the office for questioning. I'll send another car back for you in twenty minutes or so." Once again, Ronnie was doing me a favour as, although rested, I was still pretty winded myself and a slow walk would do me some good.

About an hour later I ended up back at the office. I met Ronnie half way down the hall to the cells. Ronnie was not amused.

"You son of a bitch!" he shouted. "Some partner you are, I try to do you a favour and get shit on for it!"

"What are you talking about," I ventured.

"Are you telling me you didn't know that Frankie shit his pants when you threatened to shoot him on the fence? I've spent the better part of the last hour questioning him in a tiny interview room while trying to hold down my lunch!"

"No, of course I didn't know," I replied as I started to giggle. "But now that you mention it, I did think maybe he'd cut a fart just as I put him in the car. Sorry partner!"

"Sorry don't even start to cut it," said Ronnie. "I'll get you for this, just you wait!"

Dead man talking!

As noted in the prologue, police officers are not the only ones on this planet who enjoy practical jokes. However, it's rare that individuals unwittingly play a practical joke on themselves.

A friend of mine was training to be a paramedic. His family owned a funeral home; so he was training to be an undertaker also. Part of his training for one or the other of these pursuits was a stint working in the morgue of a large hospital.

While on such duties, Jack received a call to go to Room 504 to pick up an elderly gentleman who'd just taken his last breath. It had been a long day, and Jack had been run off his feet for most of his shift. That might be why he got off the elevator on the wrong floor and ended up in Room 405. There he found an elderly gent lying quietly on a gurney, already partially sedated and ready to be wheeled off for surgery. Jack kicked the wheel-locks off the gurney and headed for the service elevator. When he reached the basement level—morgues always seem to be in basements—he rolled the gurney out of the elevator and down the hallway. The lights cast ominous shadows in various nooks and crannies of the century-old hospital as Jack wheeled his latest client towards the cutting room.

"Them basement hallways always did give me the willies," Jack explained many months later.

In one of the alcoves Jack passed were several snack machines. As he manoeuvred the gurney up against the far wall, Jack jokingly remarked to his "recently deceased" passenger, "I guess you won't mind if I grab a coffee, right?"

"Not at all," replied the elderly gent as he awakened groggily from his nap.

"I damn near shit myself," Jack admitted. "The old guy was already half sedated so I rushed him back to his room before the surgery orderly arrived. That old fart is sure lucky. He'll never know just how close he ended up under the pathologist's knife!"

"What about the fellow in Room 504," I asked.

"Oh, he was a piece of cake – much quieter," smiled Jack.

Want a light?

My friend Jack finally passed all the required training and became both a full-fledged paramedic and a qualified undertaker. His family's funeral practice was in an isolated rural area with only one ambulance. As a result, when the emergency vehicle was in for repair, one of the funeral parlor's hearses did double-duty as an ambulance.

One dark night, one of the local yahoos drove his souped-up Mustang into a tree and killed himself. After detailing the scene, my partner Ronnie and I waited soberly for Jack to arrive. Before long, up drove this huge black hearse. Jack had brought his kid brother along with him for company on the long drive back to the closest morgue situated in a nearby city. Although the particulars of the accident appeared clear-cut, we still needed an autopsy to check for alcohol or illicit drugs and to confirm the cause of death. Just before Jack closed the hearse's tailgate, my partner, Ronnie, slipped into the vehicle to maintain continuity of possession of the deceased as until formally released to the pathologist the body was considered police evidence. Joey, was already seated in the front passenger seat, so Jack slipped behind the wheel and headed for the highway.

"I was doing about sixty miles an hour," Jack related to me later; "when Joey tapped out a cigarette, popped it between his lips, and leaned over and asked me for a light."

"No problem," came Ronnie's gruff voice from the back of the hearse, his arm reaching into the front seat while he flicked open his lighter.

"Lord-fuck-a-duck," said Jack, laughing. "Luckily I caught the sleeve of Joey's jacket as he opened the side door to jump out of Old Betsy! I'd never seen him move so fast, or look so white, or be so mad! Your partner was splitting a gut in the back seat while my brother swore like a pirate up front!"

"Hey, all I did was offer the kid a light," said Ronnie later, with a grin.

Malachite green

Modern police use a wide range of tools to protect the innocent and collar the guilty. Today, most members of the public have heard about fingerprints and DNA, but not too many are aware of "malachite green."

Think of the finest powder imaginable, paired with a tenacious resistance to most cleaning products; then color that powder a bright shade of emerald. That's what law enforcement officers used to call "malachite green." According to some sources, Malachite crystals had been ground into powder and worn as eye makeup as far back as 3000 BC. Malachite has also been dubbed "The Magic Stone" for it is said to bring its wearer good luck, safe travel, and general protection. Well, such wasn't the case in my day as we used it to catch criminals with sticky-fingers. You know the ones; those digits which seem to sneak into tiny nooks, crannies, pockets and the odd desk drawer where they have absolutely no legitimate reason to be. Once stained by malachite green, however, the owner of those sticky fingers ran out of luck pretty quickly.

The label on the bottle advised users to avoid breathing malachite green dust; to wear protective gloves, clothing and respirator; and if at all possible, to avoid air movement when dispensing this powder. All good advice as this anecdote will explain.

The place we used this dust most frequently was in desk drawers. When a teacher or office worker complained about missing change or other small items, we'd apply a small amount of the powder to the inside of one of their desk drawers, the one where they usually kept their valuables. The desk's owner would then leave a small amount of money as bait and refrain from using the drawer. We then asked them to check the drawer frequently. Once they realized the money was gone, they'd call us back in. As mentioned, malachite green resisted most common cleaning products and indeed, normal efforts to remove it just ground the crystals of the powder deeper into one's skin. So we'd line up the entire class or staff and check their hands. The one with bright green fingers usually confessed in short order.

So much for the official use of malachite green; the unofficial use of this stuff was; however, way more fun!

A favourite trick was to apply a small amount of powder to the inside of a fellow officer's police cap. Once they put the cap back on the damage started. The more they perspired, the more spectacular the result. When the cap came off, their forehead was stained a bright green. Sometimes, if everyone played along quietly, the victim might walk around for hours blissfully unaware of their predicament. They'd walk around town and wonder why members of the public were staring at them so strangely.

Another prank was to dust a little powder on someone's typewriter keys. Yes, this was long before the

---

arrival of modern computers and keyboards. This was actually quite mean as the victim ended up spending hours and hours cleaning and re-cleaning the machine in question.

One day, after using the powder, someone accidentally left the open jar on an open windowsill. Later that day, people started complaining of being pranked. Usually, the prankster fessed up quite quickly as there was always a certain amount of glory and bragging rights attached to catching a co-worker with their pants down. Not on this occasion, however. Everyone professed innocence. Finally, somebody spied the open jar on the windowsill.

The office clean-up lasted for days and days!

CSI – not!

Back in the days when police drove standard gear-shifted, black and white cruisers, and concluded many cases with a kind word or stern warning; the public was largely ignorant of modern crime scene identification methods. Not like today when, thanks to television and movies, many citizens are as fine-tuned to the latest forensic techniques as most police officers.

However, the use of fingerprints to identify criminals has been around since the early 1900s, so even backwoods rednecks had heard about such stuff when I was a young cop. Heard about it—yes; mastered the concept—no!

Sergeant Freddie Simpson and I were called to a scene of damage to property. On arrival, the lady of the house led us into her living room and pointed to a large hole in her picture window. She then pointed out a sizable rock lying on the carpet near her couch.

"It came out of nowhere!" she told us frantically. "One minute I was watching my soaps and then the next minute—whammo!"

I asked the lady if she'd had any trouble with neighbors; if anyone had threatened her recently; if she'd received any strange phone calls—all the usual stuff. The veteran Sergeant Simpson stepped outside to look around and check for footprints in her garden. When he returned, I was midstream into explaining the poor-to-impossible chances of us finding the perpetrator.

"But what about fingerprints?" asked the lady, pointing to the still muddy rock lying on the floor. Before I could think how to tell the poor soul that fingerprints don't adhere to rough—let alone wet, muddy surfaces—Freddie came to my rescue.

"Of course! How could we have forgotten to check for prints? Thank goodness you're on the ball lady," he said with a smile. "Hand me your fingerprint spectrometer, Wyatt."

"My what?" I replied, totally confused.

"Your fingerprint spectrometer!" he continued, pointing to my large black & orange flashlight. "You know, the orange cone-shaped tool attached to the end of your forensic analyzer."

"My, uh, forensic analyzer?" I managed to stammer, "You mean this thing?" I unhooked the fluorescent plastic cone from the business end of my trusty traffic flashlight.

"Thanks, Wyatt," Freddie continued with a smile, "I left mine in the car."

Freddie proceeded to get down on all fours and, using the cone like a portable microscope, he examined the muddy rock from all sides. Finally, after what seemed like hours—but was no doubt closer to mere seconds—he rose to his feet while shaking his head sadly from side to side.

"Nope, no such luck! I guess the person who threw this rock was wearing gloves or wiped the rock clean before he threw it. We may be dealing with that serious customer we've been after for several weeks now. His name's 'Rocky,' isn't that it Officer Holmes?"

"Uh, yeah, I think that's it Sarg! Yes, that's definitely it—Rocky!" I replied, finally catching on.

"Well, at least you checked!" nodded the elderly lady as she smiled at my sergeant and then threw a wicked frown in my direction, "It's nice to know some people know how to do their jobs and still care about us senior citizens."

"Have a nice day Ma'am!" said Sergeant Simpson with a chuckle, as we headed back to our cruiser.

A burning issue

When I made the grade to detective, I was sent on a surveillance course. It didn't take long to find out everything I'd been doing wrong for so many years.

First I learned that following someone on foot was quite different from vehicle-to-vehicle surveillance. Following someone on foot is much harder than following a vehicle, as the target is smaller—person vs. vehicle— and a savvy criminal can slip away in a heartbeat if not followed with care and at least some level of expertise.

Next I learned that seasoned targets routinely conducted counter-surveillance. I learned not to order anything hot, like coffee, after tailing a target suspect into a restaurant. If suspicious, a suspect might order a hot meal; and then pay and leave the restaurant just as his lunch or dinner arrived. Then they'd check to see if anyone else departed in a hurry, leaving a hot drink or meal on their table—a sure sign of a "tail." If alone, I learned to sit at the restaurant counter—if it had one—as a single person sitting at a table or in a booth is more conspicuous.

I also learned to watch my target indirectly, such as in the semi-mirrored surfaces of store windows. Direct eye contact was definitely frowned upon. Elevators posed other challenges. Again, a smart target might get on an elevator and then jump off just before the doors closed. This often resulted in the police-tail doing "the-green-apple-two-step" as we called it. That's when the police surveillance operator hesitates as to whether to stay on or get off the elevator—another sure sign of surveillance. The same goes for buses, trains and subways.

Clothing is also important. Too formal or too casual doesn't allow the watcher to enter all venues comfortably. "Business casual" was the dress of choice for the practiced operator. Removing a jacket, or adding a tie, hat or raincoat, can do wonders to change one's appearance. All these tricks should be intuitive, especially after watching all the police shows on TV; but it was good to practice them in a controlled environment all the same. I also learned to expect the unexpected; something my buddy Dean missed somehow.

We were about thirty officers on this training course and penalties for mistakes usually took the form of paying for coffee or beer later in the day. As noted earlier, surveillance is conducted in teams so any mistakes usually resulted in team penalties. One team on the course bought beverages quite frequently, usually because of just one of their team members. That's right, his name was Dean.

Dean was a solid police officer, but he just didn't seem to be cut out for surveillance. He'd make full eye contact or bump into targets more than anyone else and had raised the-green-apple-two-step to heights approaching a veritable art form. His team mates helped him at first; then later harassed him mercilessly, all to no avail. One day, one of his colleagues gained the team's revenge.

We were on an afternoon break in a rather large downtime-room. People stood standing around chatting, sipping coffee or catching up on their notes. Dean was sitting on a low couch reading a newspaper. He had the paper right up against his nose so was pretty oblivious to things going on directly in front of him. Without warning, one of Dean's team mates quietly dropped to his knees and snuck up on him. He then flicked his lighter and set the bottom edge of Dean's newspaper on fire. A small flame crawled slowly along the bottom edge of the day's news. Dean must have been reading the top of the page, because he casually raised his head and asked obliviously, "Does anyone smell smoke?"

The room erupted in riotous laughter. Dean, still oblivious to his urgent predicament continued.

"Seriously guys, I smell smoke!" Just then the flames blossomed up the sides of the paper scorching his fingers. "What the hell?" screamed Dean as he threw the paper to the floor and started stamping on it vigorously.

"Looks like you got some 'hot news' there, Dean!" laughed one officer.

"Okay, very funny!" he shouted. Then, after the fire was out, "Okay you assholes; who's the bastard that lit-up my paper?" Silence reigned. Just then, the course supervisor re-entered the room.

"Does anyone smell smoke?" he asked, innocently.

Once again, the room burst into laughter!

Revenge is sweet

One thing about practical jokes is that they sometimes have a way of coming back to bite you! Such was the case for one fellow I knew many years ago.

Rob was well known and well liked as a police officer. One of his many attributes was an active sense of humor. He was usually ready to tell a joke or funny story and always ready to plan, participate and perpetrate a good practical joke. One day he called the local newspaper.

"Hi there," he said. "I'd like to place an ad in your classified section. The ad should read as follows: '21 cubic inch refrigerator for sale; only 3 weeks old; $50 or best offer; call Fred at 123-4567.'" Fred, of course didn't have a fridge for sale, especially one at such an unbelievably low price. What Fred did have, however, was a home phone number listed locally as 123-4567. Rob had checked the listing twice as he carefully prepared his prank.

As soon as Rob's ad appeared in the classifieds, Fred's phone started to ring.

"Hello? What's that? A fridge for sale? No, I'm sorry; there must be some mistake. No, I don't have a fridge for sale."

"Hello? What did you say? Sorry buddy, I don't have a fridge for sale—bye!."

"Hello? What? A brand new fridge for $50? I think someone's yanking your chain buddy. What? In the newspaper? With my phone number? Are you kidding me?" By this time, of course, Fred was starting to smell a rat. "No, no, no; I'm not obliged to sell you my new fridge 'cause I don't have a new fridge and besides, my old one's worth a lot more than fifty bucks! Yeah, well—the same to you buddy!" Fred shouted at the last caller, as he slammed down the phone.

Fred's phone, of course, just kept ringing, and ringing, and ringing. Morning, noon and night, his phone rang incessantly—until he finally left it off the hook and then arranged with the phone company to have his number changed. After that ordeal, all Fred wanted to do was identify the prankster so he could seek revenge. However, Rob had acted alone on this particular joke and had told not a soul about what he'd done. Despite his best efforts, Fred simply couldn't identify his antagonist.

Several months later, however, Rob had a beer or three too many and, human nature being what it is, he spilled the beans to a casual acquaintance. Before long, the story spread to all and sundry, yes—even to Fred.

Fred had worked in the same town for years and years. He'd made many friends and perhaps a few enemies. However, suffice it to say that Fred was "well connected." The following morning, Rob prepared to head for work.

"See you later, Honey!" he shouted to his wife over his shoulder as he opened the door from the kitchen to the garage. He walked to the rear of his car and grabbed the handle and opened his exterior garage door.

"What the fuck!" he blurted suddenly.

Sitting in his driveway was a boulder the size of a small planet—well, perhaps more of a rock the size of a small SUV. Regardless, he couldn't back his car out of his garage to get to work. Heck, he couldn't move his car at all before the obstacle was removed. Yeah, Fred knew people alright. During the night, a couple of his landscaping buddies had paid Rob's home a visit.

Fred wasn't much of a drinker and never did spill his own beans about the rock, so Rob never did find out for sure who had gotten some payback—Rob had certainly pranked lots of people over the years. The rest of us, however, had our suspicions.

None of us will ever know what it cost Fred to have the rock delivered—probably nothing more than calling in a couple of past favours. But we all heard loud and clear what it cost Rob to get the rock removed—a bundle!

The muffler bites back

As detectives, Garth and I frequently found ourselves driving between one town and another in pursuit of interviews, investigative leads or other evidence. Our unmarked cruiser was a late model, puke-green, four door sedan.

One day, Garth says to me, "Watch this, Wyatt!" He then proceeded—at 60 mph—to turn off the ignition key. A few seconds later, with our automatic transmission still in "D" for drive and speeding down the highway; he turned the key on again. Suddenly, the car jerked as the muffler emitted an ear-splitting explosive BANG!

"What the heck was that?" I asked.

"Damned if I know how it works, but my cousin's a mechanic and told me to try it out—pretty cool, eh?"

"It may be cool," I replied, but it can't be doing the muffler much good.

"Nah, my cousin said it's harmless. Anyway, to heck with the muffler," Garth continued, "Just think of the fun we can have scaring the shit out of people up and down our normally boring old highway!"

"You're crazy!" I countered. "You know you're really certifiably crazy, right?" Garth just laughed, as he switched the key off and on again to produce another enormous backfire—essentially a "car-fart."

Well, despite my initial misgivings, Garth and I spent the rest of the week "farting" our muffler. We quickly learned that the technique was fairly simple: attain cruising speed, switch the key off, wait a second or two, then switch the key back on and—BOOM! It worked like a charm every time. We found that the longer we coasted before turning the key back on the larger and louder the fart. The best fun came in the timing of each fart; as they say in real estate—location—location—location! Farting in the open countryside quickly became boring. So we started making our vehicle fart in built up areas, preferably where some type of crowd had gathered. Highway workers were easy prey as they laboured away behind their large orange traffic cones. We'd build up a little speed and then coast up until just level with a work crew—then BANG! Boy, those guys sure knew how to jump! Fellows working on bridges and overpasses were… well, that's another story. However, as the saying goes, all good things must come to an end sometime.

On a lazy fall afternoon, we spied a group of kids walking home from school. Garth was driving so gave me the nod as he turned off the key. When he turned it on again, the regular BANG we were used to was followed by a high-pitched squealing sound coming from beneath our vehicle.

"Jesus-H-Christ," said Garth, "What the hell is that?"

It sounded a little like slowly letting the air out of a birthday balloon, only much, much louder. The squeal continued as we quickly made our way to a muffler & brake shop close by. When the mechanic got our car up on his hoist, he let out a whistle.

"Holy shit, I've never seen a muffler like this one before!" He called to his colleagues, "Hey boys, take a look at this!" The other mechanics gathered around and exchanged puzzled glances. Slowly, all eyes turned to Garth and I.

"Any idea what happened here officers?" asked our mechanic.

"Nope," said Garth innocently. "The darn thing just went bang and started squealing. So we figured we'd better get it in and have it checked."

"Well, come over here and take a look for yourselves. It's as if someone let off a hand grenade inside your muffler." We both leaned down under the car and saw what he meant. The poor muffler did indeed look like it'd been blown up from the inside out. It was covered with bumps slightly reminiscent of a turtle's shell.

"Well, just fix it and hand us the bill," I said.

"Don't you want us to send the bill direct to the city as usual?" asked the mechanic with the start of a smile.

"Naw, we'll take care of it," mumbled Garth.

"Yeah, it's probably the least you could do," replied the mechanic knowingly.

No sleeping on my watch!

Once again, Garth and I found ourselves travelling the highways and byways between two cities. The shortest route involved a much travelled, yet boring stretch of two-lane asphalt. After a long week away in one city or another, it was always hard to stay awake at the wheel while heading home. As a result, we agreed that whoever drove, the other would help keep the driver alert.

At the end of one particularly tiring week, I lost the coin toss so settled in behind the wheel for the two hour trek home. A few minutes later, I had to shake Garth's shoulder—he'd fallen asleep and was snoring quietly up against his window.

"Hey, you're supposed to keep me awake, Bozo!" I admonished with a smile. "Turn the radio up or tell me your life story again or something!"

"Yeah, yeah," replied Garth as he settled back against the window. Not long later, I realized he was snoring again.

"Wake up, you sorry excuse for a partner," I said, shaking him again. "If I end up driving off a cliff or something it'll be all-your-fault!" My words fell on deaf ears; or at least snoozy-ears. Before long, Garth was snoring even more loudly and my eyes were getting heavier and heavier. I decided to wake Garth up again and have a little fun at the same time.

A few minutes later I spied a fully loaded tractor-trailer parked on the shoulder of the highway about a half-mile away. I took my foot off the gas and gently applied the brakes. About twenty yards shy of the rear bumper of the huge rig's trailer; I simultaneously slammed on the brakes and leaned on the horn! The tires squealed, the horn blared, and Garth shot straight up in the air screaming like a stuck pig—or at least like a body about the meet its maker by being skewered on the tailgate of a semi-trailer.

"Son of a bitch!" was one of the milder expletives Garth uttered for what seemed like the next ten minutes or so. At least it was long enough for me to get back on the highway and achieve cruising speed again. Of course I was laughing so hard I could hardly hear him.

The excitement kind of woke me up a little, and Garth's incessant complaining helped keep me that way for the remainder of our journey home.

Don't cry over smashed glass!

Some officers stay in the same role, squad or section for their entire career. Others, like me, enjoyed the variety of multiple postings. At one spot, my boss, Craig, drove a dark blue four door sedan. Although issued by the department, it was his pride and joy and he looked after it like it was a brand new, shiny Corvette. If he'd had his way, he'd have been the only one allowed to drive that particular vehicle. However, it belonged to the department so he had to lend it out on occasion, when needed. Of course, he also had to hand it over to his temporary replacement when away on business trips. As luck would have it, every time Craig returned to town it seemed that something had happened to his big blue machine.

On one occasion, the officer replacing him had a minor fender bender. On another occasion, another replacing officer was parked at a sports field when an errant baseball left a significant dent on the car's hood. It was like his stand-ins were jinxed or something.

Anyway, one day Craig arrived back from a business trip. Moe and I met him at the airport. As we walked to the parking lot, Craig's face fell one more time.

"That's not my car is it?" he asked, eyeing a large blue sedan with a sheet of plastic covering the front passenger side window. "Tell me that's not my car! Please tell me that's not my car," he pleaded.

'Yup, sorry Boss," I replied. "We had another little mishap while you were away." I helped Moe get Craig's luggage into the trunk and then jumped behind the wheel. Craig sat up front where pieces of safety glass were still stuck in the carpet. Moe jumped in the back.

"I just can't leave town without someone smashing up my beautiful car!" moaned Craig. "I gotta tell you guys, I dread coming home now—I just know I'll find some scratch, dent or broken part that wasn't there when I left town."

Now, normally, Craig would have been right. However, this time, Moe and I had set him up. We'd smashed a piece of stray safety glass and sprinkled some pieces on the front carpet. We'd then rolled down the window—a power option on his beautiful "Big Blue"—and taped on some plastic sheeting. We'd also wedged a tape recorder under the front armrest to capture any words of wisdom our redoubtable boss might feel obliged to share. The stage was set, now all we had to do was sit back, the recorder already running, and wait.

"What am I going to do with you people? Remedial driver-training might be one option, but knowing you guys you'd just go out on a high-speed chase or something," said Craig, as he went on and on for several minutes while Moe and I listened patiently.

"Okay, let's have it! Who smashed the window anyway? Wyatt, was it you? I thought you had better sense. Moe? What about you? I'll have you back rattling doorknobs by this time tomorrow!

"Oh my poor, poor car! What a bunch of idiots! How did you people even get through the academy?

"The baseball fiasco was that jerk Harry, wasn't it? And who was it the time before that—James? Poor guy can't even park straight let alone drive safely down a highway! Remedial driver training—it'd definitely be a waste on him!"

"I swear I'm going to drive the next time I head out of town so you morons don't have a chance to massacre my big blue pride and joy!

"For crying out loud, with the wind noise from this bloody plastic, I can't even hear myself think!"

Craig had just given us the opening we'd been waiting for!

"No problem, Boss," I said, as I pressed the button at my elbow to roll up the electric window on his side of the vehicle. As the window slid shut—silence reigned; but not for long.

"You sons of bitches," voiced Craig with a chuckle. "You really got me this time—you really had me going there! Okay, not a word to anyone—I want your promise boys! If this gets around I'll be a laughing stock!"

"I promise 'I' won't repeat a word to anyone, Boss. How about you, Moe, will 'You' say anything?"

"Not in a million years," came the reply from the backseat.

"Okay then, we got a deal," said Craig, as my finger hit the playback button…

"What am I going to do with you people? Remedial driver-training might be one option, but then you'd just go out on a high-speed chase or something."

Craig's eyes opened wide as his jaw dropped into his lap! The tape continued...

"Okay, let's have it! Who smashed the window anyway? Wyatt, was it you? I thought you had better sense. Moe? What about..."

"Shit, you bastards got me again!" laughed Craig. "You God-damned sons of bitches!" he blurted as we all laughed loudly. "But silence is golden boys, and we've still got a deal—right buddies?

Arthur—sit down!

As I may have mentioned, at times, rural policing really has its moments.

When Peter and I responded to one domestic dispute, we found an entire family in an uproar with two brothers slugging it out over a yet to be known private issue. It was a sprawling old farmhouse with about 15-20 people crowded around the living room watching the fun. Two dogs, three cats and a pig completed the picture— yes, a pig—and yes, all in a small living room.

"Come on fella's!" Peter shouted as we separated the two pugilists. "Let's just calm it down a notch or two!" I took one fellow to a bedroom and Peter took the other to the kitchen. Things seemed to be going well until

I heard a sharp squeal come from the other side of the spacious home. Next I heard another squeal, and it didn't sound so much like a pig. Indeed, it sounded more like my brave partner—Peter! Then the squealing intensified! I told Suspect #1 to stay put and quickly made my way to the kitchen. In one corner was Suspect #2 and in the other corner was Peter; with the now highly enraged pig nipping at his toes. I joined the fray and tugged mightily on the pig's tail trying to drag it's 100 plus pounds away from Peter.

"Call off the pig," shouted Peter. "Call it off or I'll shoot the damned thing!" I figured Peter was wasting his breath as this was a pig we were dealing with, not a trained Husky or something. Heck, even I knew that cats don't listen, so why would a pig? Just when we both thought all was lost, the farmer's wife entered the kitchen.

"Arthur! Back-off Arthur! Sit go to your corner! You heard me, go sit down!" Without further ado, Arthur—the pig—waddled over to a blanket in one corner and, with a loud closing grunt, promptly sat down. By this time, Peter and I had become the center of attention.

Before we knew it the two brothers had made up and so we let them both off with a warning.

Just to regain our sense of balance in the world, with our breakfast the next morning we each ordered an extra serving of bacon!

Some cop you are!

As mentioned earlier, my fiancée's father operated a butcher shop & general store. He usually slaughtered his own meat and everyone for miles around agreed that Nick's meat was the best!

Nick was an experienced butcher. He could guess the weight of a live animal to within a pound or two—not an easy feat when dealing with 200-400 pound swine and 800-1200 pound cattle. He could skin a steer in five minutes flat after putting the animal down from 50 feet away with his trusty .222 Magnum. However, Nick killed most of the selected animals at close range—usually from just a few feet away.

One day Nick invited me to help him go pick up a bull whose destiny included a walk-in refrigerator. Nick's routine was to position the animal near the tailgate of his truck, shoot it between the eyes, bleed it out, and then tie a braided wire cord to its neck and winch it into the back of his truck. This may sound complicated, but trying to manoeuvre a thousand pound animal up a ramp into an enclosed space is a heck of a lot easier when the beast is dead—Dead—DEAD. On this occasion, Nick invited me to do the honors in killing the bull. When we arrived at a neighboring ranch, the farmer brought an enormous animal out of a barn and positioned it about a dozen yards from the tailgate. I didn't need to be an expert in animals to know that this was the biggest, most bad-assed bull I'd ever seen. I figured it must have weighed at least two or three tons; heck the horns alone must have weighed more than most large dogs. I raised the rifle up to my shoulder and prepared to shoot. Well, shooting with a scope is fine if your target is at a distance, but at 30 feet, I quickly realized that the scope just gets in the way.

"Okay, Wyatt," Nick said, "He's ready—shoot! Hit him right between the eyes, boy. Go for it!"

Aiming down the side of the barrel, I let one round loose. The .222 Magnum didn't have much of a kick, certainly less than the rifles I was used to. I figured at this range I couldn't miss—wrong! When I looked up over the scope, the bull was still standing. A small trickle of blood oozed out of the right side of the bull's massive head. I couldn't believe I'd missed him! The bull shook its head and snorted loudly.

"Shoot him again, Wyatt!" shouted Nick with a chuckle.

"Yeah, boy, shoot again," joined in the farmer, still holding the bull's bridle nervously.

My second shot hit the bull's forehead on the left side of its white blaze and prompted an expressive grunt. The bull then started snorting in earnest as he started to paw the ground beneath him.

"That boy's gonna get us all killed!" screamed the farmer, as he dropped the rope and jumped behind the barn door.

"Give me that thing," shouted Nick, as he grabbed his trusty rifle back—no chuckle this time. In one fluid motion, Nick raised the carbine up to his shoulder and pulled the trigger. BANG! Down went the bull like a sack of potatoes.

"Some cop you are," said Nick with a snort of his own, "Can't even hit a twelve-hundred and twenty-three pound bull at ten paces!"

"Yeah, some cop!" mimicked the farmer.

For some reason, Nick never asked me to help shoot animals again.

Dead shot Wyatt!

No, Nick never asked me to shoot a domestic animal again. However, he did one day goad me into joining him to hunt deer.

It was a quiet week at his butcher shop so Nick, now my father-in-law, suggested we go hunting. Focused on regaining my honor after failing to kill a tied-up 1223 pound bull, I readily agreed. Our quarry on this occasion was to be white-tailed deer. They're a good sized animal and one we'd have to shoot from a distance. I figured scope-or-not, this would be a walk in the park!

We picked a gorgeous fall day in the middle of the local deer hunting season. With a couple of packed lunches, we headed out into the wilderness in Nick's trusty old pick-me-up truck. Nick brought along his 30:30 Remington and I borrowed a .308 Winchester from my office. I'd used the Winchester before during annual firearms qualifications and, without Nick's knowledge I'd taken the time to sight it in properly a few days before our adventure.

I guess there are many different ways to hunt deer. In our neck of the woods there were sufficient deer and enough abandoned logging roads that all one had to do was drive along slowly for a few hours and wait for a deer to wander into your rifle sights. However, Nick and I agreed that such practice was hardly sporting; so we parked the truck and started walking. Nick of course led the way. After an hour or so, we spied a couple of deer foraging through an area of clear-cut; a logging area where all the trees & brush had been cut down and the stumps ground into the soil by huge machines called, you guessed it—"crushers." Sounds pretty unpleasant, but the crushing action facilitates replanting for effective reforestation.

"Want to take a shot?" asked Nick.

"No thanks, I think they're too far for a sure kill," I replied. "I'd rather not wound the poor things and then have to chase them for miles & miles through the damn brush."

"Good call," replied Nick with a smile.

Still leading the way, Nick led us up over a hill and down into a pleasant valley.

"How about taking out a partridge before we head for home?" Nick enquired with a smile.

"A partridge?" I replied. "But all we have are large calibre rifles, don't you usually use small bore shotguns for partridges."

"Well, normally—yes," said Nick with a smile. "But I see a partridge down the road a-ways who's just itching to be invited for dinner!" I followed his gaze down the dirt road we'd been following and spied the partridge—a mere speck in the distance. "I bet you can't hit that bird from here!" Nick challenged.

Sliding a shell into the rifle's breach, I took careful aim and let off one round. The speck in the distance jumped into the air and then disappeared.

"You missed him," laughed Nick.

"I don't think so," I replied, grinning from ear to ear. "Let's go see."

As we got closer we could see that the partridge was indeed lying dead on the roadway. Upon closer examination, we found the poor bird's head completely obliterated. We both agreed that due to the high velocity of the bullet even the slipstream of a near miss might have caused the damage. As I carefully placed the dead bird in my haversack, Nick started laughing.

"What's so funny? I asked, "The bird's dead so I win the challenge don't I?" Nick nodded in reply, but could not find his voice as he was bent over laughing so hard. He finally straightened up and pointed to a sign we'd both missed seeing on the side of the road. It seems the deer weren't the only ones who had wandered. The sign said, "No Hunting—Game Preserve."

"Some cop you are," Nick laughed. "You can now add illegal hunting to your resume. Oh, didn't I tell you? Partridge season ended two weeks ago!"

Doggie on a roll

Arnold was a good cop and he loved a good prank, even if some of his jokes were a bit on the mean side.

One day while driving down a familiar country road, we passed a farmhouse where a large black dog had a habit of running out to chase anything with wheels down the highway.

"That dog's going to kill someone someday!" Arnold announced gravely.

"What do you mean," I replied with surprise, "He's harmless."

"One of these days, he's going to distract a nervous driver and make him drive into the ditch or, worse yet, into the path of another vehicle for a head-on collision."

"Being a little dramatic today, aren't you, Arnold?"

"Nope, Wyatt—just realistic. Maybe we should teach the mutt a little lesson. Turn around and drive by the farmhouse again." he said.

So I turned the car around and drove by again. This time the dog was on my side of our marked police car, yet he still ran out into the road nipping at the rear tires of our vehicle.

"One more time," said Arnold.

So I turned around again and headed back up the lonely two-lane byway.

"Not too fast," cautioned Arnold, "About 20-25 mph should do the trick."

As we approached the dog's driveway I could see him crouching down in a starter's stance. When we came level with the farmhouse, out he came like a flash! Before I realized what had happened, Arnold had opened his door and caught the poor dog with a broadside blow that bowled the poor beast right off of its feet and into the ditch.

"That should do the trick!" smiled Arnold. "Let's drive by just one last time to see if he's learned anything."

This time the dog met us at the end of its driveway barking loudly—but he never set a foot off his master's property.

"Works every time," chuckled Arnold. "Next time I'll drive and you can play doorman!"

Bomb scare at the high school

Some practical jokes are initiated on the spur of the moment and take mere seconds to complete. Others, however, take careful thought and serious planning. Such was the case one quiet spring afternoon in our small, lazy location east of the meandering Mississippi and north of the mighty Susquehanna.

A bunch of officers were sitting around the squad room having a quiet coffee. That's when Henry mentioned that one of his buddies had just graduated from the regional police academy and had secured a position at a neighboring town.

"He said he'd stop in and stay with me for a couple of days en route. He's fully trained, but still pretty green.

Let's have a little fun with him. Any ideas boys?" After brainstorming various options, Ralph came up with a novel prank—one we'd never tried before.

"Let's blow him up!" suggested Ralph.

"Blow him up?" several co-workers gasped in unison.

"Sure! Here's how it'll go down." Ralph proceeded to outline his plan. Everyone agreed and after a few precious tweaks the die was cast.

Henry's friend was arriving around supper time. We knew his buddy would be anxious for a ride-along, so Henry made sure both he and the rookie, Daniel, would be available in Unit 5 when the call went out. Meanwhile, we taped together five red traffic flares with black electrical tape and inserted wires at both ends of the bundle. We twisted the tips of these wires together loosely and bound them with another small piece of tape. The "bomb" looked pretty convincing, even to our seasoned eyes. Jack was the scruffiest amongst us so he agreed to play the "criminal element" of this little jest. Taking our taped-up creation with him, Jack went home to change into his grubbiest clothes. He then proceeded to the local high school, now closed for the day.

"Make sure all firearms are empty," Ralph had cautioned, "Especially yours Henry; and make sure your buddy hasn't watched too many Dirty Harry movies. We don't want him whipping out a personal piece."

"No problem!" Henry smiled, "This is going to be a night to remember!"

As soon as Jack was in place behind the school, the call went out.

"Unit 5, Unit 5; respond to complaint of a suspicious person out back of the high school. It may be nothing. The night janitor's a little nervous after that bomb scare at a school in Naybortown last week."

"Roger that," replied Henry over his police radio. A couple of minutes later another call was issued. The dispatcher sounded excited—what an actor!

"Unit 5, Unit 5, proceed with caution. The janitor called again and he thinks the guy has a bomb or something. Unit 2, I know you're a plain clothes unit, but can you provide backup? Over?"

"Unit 2 here, 10-4, we'll be there in three minutes." I replied. Normally, detectives were called in after the fact, but heck, we wanted in on the fun too.

"Uh, Unit 5 here, I've got an unarmed ride-along with me. He's a new officer headed for Naybortown. Should I drop him off before arriving at the scene?"

"Negative, Unit 5. Just make sure he stays in the car. We don't want Naybortown's chief down our throats for losing one of his officers before he's even on the payroll."

"Roger that. Unit 5 arriving at the school now; we'll take a look and let you know the score." A pregnant silence followed before the next radio call.

"Dispatch, this is Unit 5. It's a bomb alright. We're around the back of the school and have the suspect in our headlights. He's crouched down by the cafeteria wall and looks like he's holding several sticks of dynamite. Unit 2, where are you?"

"Right behind you, Unit 5. We'll ditch the car in front and walk around. We've got you covered. What's your next move?"

"Time to talk him down, I guess," said Henry, before climbing out of his cruiser. Ralph and I joined him about thirty feet from the "mad bomber" with empty guns in hand. Despite being warned to stay in the car, Daniel slipped out of Unit 5 and crept up to join us. *Oh, don't you just love it when a plan comes together!*

"What's going on, friend," said Henry, as he commenced to talk Jack down. Jack should have gotten an Oscar that evening as he played the mad bomber role to perfection. He explained how the teachers hated him when he was younger and how, at the still juvenile age of seventeen, he was expelled for smoking weed and throwing a meal tray at a cafeteria worker. After leaving school, he said he'd spent time in a mental institution and then on release worked in construction. However, he'd never forgotten the humiliation he'd suffered at this here school. Now it was time for some payback. He explained how he'd stolen the dynamite from his jobsite and had rigged it to blow him and the school to heaven or hell—he didn't much care which. Henry too should have gotten some type of honorable mention as supporting cast. After some tense minutes, he got Jack to the brink of giving up and letting a doctor back at "the home" check him out.

"Okay," said Jack quietly, "I'll give up my dynamite, but not to you. I'll only hand it over to the guy back there without the uniform." As I started to walk slowly forward, Jack spoke again—loudly.

"No, not the fat bald guy. To the young guy in the jeans and t-shirt." We all turned around and stared at Henry's friend, Daniel.

"You don't have to do this," Ralph said with eyes of steel.

"Uh, no problem," stammered Daniel uncertainly. "I can handle this—he's giving up, right?" As we all nodded, including Jack, Daniel crept forward carefully.

"Take it easy, fellow," said Daniel. "Just give me the dynamite and we'll take care of both it and you. It'll all be over soon! Those nice doctors are going to take care of you real good." As he got closer, Jack slowly stood up.

"Okay, I'm ready. But this stuff's really unstable so be careful. Put out your hands palms up and I'll place the bomb on them. Just be careful not to separate the two wires on top. If you do—BANG!—we're all gonners! There's enough dynamite here to take out most of the school and half the forest behind you!" Daniel tip-toed the last few steps with his palms outstretched awaiting "the bomb." Just as Jack placed the weight of the package in Daniel's hands, he grabbed both wires and, jerking them apart, shouted…

"BYE BYE—SUCKERS!"

Daniel didn't move a muscle! He watched as Jack fell to all fours laughing hysterically.

"Okay, get him boys!" said Daniel shakily.

"What are you waiting for?" he continued as he turned slowly in our direction, still being very careful not to jiggle the bomb. "It looks like a dud, but you never know and… hey, what's going on?" None of us could help him, of course, as we were all bent over laughing our guts out.

"It's a joke? It's a God-damned joke!" screamed Daniel. "It can't be—it's a real bomb for Christ's sake!"

Needless to say, it took us the better part of the next hour to calm Daniel down. A visit to one of our local watering holes helped, but he was still shaking, even after several formidable rum and cokes. However, with Henry's persuasion, he finally accepted that he'd been had and had good. Then, as any real cop would do, he vowed to get his revenge.

I suppose we should have been content to let this little sleeping rookie lie peacefully. However, a few weeks later, we doctored up a fake certificate for successful completion of a "Basic Bomb Disposal" course and mailed it off. Did we mail it to Daniel? No, that would have been too easy. We mailed it to the Chief of the Naybortown Police Department for formal presentation to the successful candidate!

We never did hear how Daniel made out and we're all still waiting for Daniel's revenge!

The mystical-moose-call

Sheriff Butcher was a big man. Not tall—just BIG. Not corpulent—just BIG. Big hands, big head, big shoulders, big voice – BIG! When Sheriff Butcher played a practical joke on you, you laughed. You didn't get angry—you laughed. You didn't get pouty—you laughed. You didn't even try to get even—you just laughed it off. That's just the way it was. He was that BIG.

To be honest, Sheriff Butcher's jokes were usually pretty funny. Some were even quite elaborate. Take for example his "mystical-moose-call."

As "County Mounties" in a small town along the Appalachian Mountain Range, we found various ways to entertain ourselves. Sheriff Butcher, however, took self-entertainment to new heights. After tiring of shooting flies off the office ceiling with his BB gun, he invented his very own moose-call. Everyone around was familiar with moose—those huge ugly creatures with expansive antler racks. Everyone was also familiar with hunting moose and the use of moose-calls to entice the beasts to slaughter.

Just like any other dumb animal, most moose will respond to the right call. Commercially made calls can be bought off the shelf of your local hardware or outfitter store. Others are handmade, and some seasoned hunters can call a moose with nothing other than the gifts God gave them. Call often and consistently enough and a moose will literally walk right into the sights of your high powered rifle; sometimes so close that you'd wish you'd taken the super-duper scope off the damn thing—but you're already familiar with that particular problem.

Well, Sheriff Butcher was of the "make-it-yourself" persuasion; although his prey of choice wasn't exactly moose! "If you're gonna hunt," he said later, "You want to hunt something challenging—something with a mind of its own—like your fellow man!" No, the good sheriff wasn't hell bent on dropping a criminal or two at three-hundred yards—although the thought probably passed through his mind from time to time. What he did want was to catch friends and co-workers off guard with his own devious little practical joke. So he made a moose-call.

The "Butcher Moose-call" was a work of art. He moulded it out of a ball of plaster of Paris and several feet of cut-up aluminum and copper pipes. Once finished, the call looked like an irregular-shaped softball with short pieces of pipe sticking out all over the exterior. Pieces of grass and dried fur were dutifully glued on as camouflage. The sizes of pipe varied from a quarter-inch to one inch. Some pieces were cut square, some on angles and some were flared at the end. Two pieces of pipe stood out from the others of course. One was a piece of quarter-inch pipe about nine inches long and curved downwards then upwards in a graceful arc, ending in what was obviously a mouthpiece. The other was on the opposite side and curved up and forward, ending in a trumpet-like flare.

"You just blow real hard in the mouthpiece and wait for the closest moose to come a-calling!" he'd explain to anyone willing to listen. And listen people did—in droves!

More thoughtful and less gullible folk would have taken the time to ask more questions and submit the weird looking apparatus to closer examination. But trusting the good Sheriff, each one simply picked it up, took a deep breath, and blew. "POOF"... the blower was instantly covered with fine white powder which turned out to be flour or icing sugar or anything else the good sheriff had at hand.

What Sheriff Butcher didn't tell his intended victims was that the mouthpiece wasn't connected to the trumpet-like pipe on the opposite side. Instead, the mouthpiece curved back within the ball of plaster to aim directly at the blower's nose!

Doctors, lawyers, merchants, chiefs—other chiefs—Butcher got them all. Each in turn was then duly sworn to secrecy so the joke kept getting better and better as people came to our office asking to see "the moose-call."

"The Mayor told me it was the funniest thing he'd heard in a long time," said one unsuspecting soul.

"Butcher's gonna clean-up if he ever markets that thing at Walmart," offered a local lawyer—ready to assist in the copyrighting process no doubt. In fact, many former victims accompanied co-workers, friends and neighbors to our office so they could try out the moose-call—and witness their own victims be taken down!

Eventually, of course, the word got out and the flood turned into a trickle and then died off completely. But what fun it was while it lasted. Butcher wasn't a native of our town and it is said he took it home and even got his mother to cover herself with flour. He's probably still looking over his shoulder waiting for the dime to drop—'cause the apple doesn't fall far from the tree, right? We can only hope Mamma don't use malachite green powder in *her* moose-call!

Please touch me!

Vincent worked in administration. It seemed like he'd been around forever. Folks used to say he was as old as dirt. When he finally retired, he decided to play a practical joke on the entire headquarters staff.

Over the span of several weeks, Vincent made secret bets with many of his co-workers. Indeed, he got better than three-to-one odds from some co-workers.

At Vincent's retirement party, the boss and several others gave the standard speeches accompanied by the usual presentation of gifts. Vincent wasn't known as a flamboyant character so people were quite surprised at the turnout for his parting. It seemed like everyone in the division had attended. Finally, it was Vincent's turn to address those gathered. After offering his appreciation to all and sundry, Vincent asked the boss's secretary to come forward.

Shirley was bright-eyed and buxom. She was quite young and, if the truth be told, she wasn't the brightest bulb in our division. However, she had a courteous phone manner and typed faster than anyone else around. She also had a bit of the devil in her. Vincent had obviously taken his time and had chosen his unsuspecting partner wisely.

"Shirley," said Vincent, "You've been a big help to me over the past few years. Both of us know that every time you paged me to meet with the Chief it seemed to take forever for me to show up; but you never complained. We also know that some folk think of me as the division's resident absent-minded professor who ambles up and down the hallways like a turtle late for his own root canal; but you always treated me with nothing but respect. Well, I must admit my legs don't get me around as fast as they used to do, but my hands—now that's another story.

"When I was younger I was known to have the fastest hands of any man alive. In fact, my hands are still so fast that I'll bet you I can touch your bosom and you won't even feel it."

"Ah, Vincent," Shirley laughed with a perky smile, "Don't be silly!"

"Girl, I'm dead serious and I'll put my money where my mouth is." Laying a ten dollar bill on an adjacent table Vincent continued, "I'll only touch you once, but if you feel my fingers on your body in any way, shape or manner, then this here ten dollars is yours!"

"I don't know," wavered Shirley.

"Heck, let's make it twenty bucks," smiled Vincent, as he laid down another bill.

"Only one touch?" asked Shirley.

"One touch only – and you won't even know it's happened or the money's yours!"

At this point, the Chief intervened. "Vincent, I'm, not sure where you're going with this, but maybe Shirley don't appreciate it too much."

"No, Chief," stammered Shirley. "I can take it. You're on, old timer—do your worst!"

All eyes were on Vincent as he circled around Shirley carefully. He flexed his fingers and wiggled them briskly in the air. Folk could hear him cracking his knuckles from the back of the room.

"Oh, maybe this isn't such a good idea after all," said Vincent. "Maybe I've lost my touch and I'll make a fool of myself and lose my twenty bucks."

"Hey, a bet is a bet, Vincent," coaxed Shirley gleefully. "Don't tell me you're going to chicken out! Come on, I dare you to give it a try! If you don't, I'm keeping the twenty dollars anyway!"

"Okay, okay; just give me a minute," said Vincent. Shaking the tension out of his hands one last time, he reached forward and gently fondled Shirley's breasts.

"Aghhh," screamed Shirley, "I felt that! I felt ALL of that!"

"Okay," replied Vincent with a smile, "I guess I'm not as fast as I thought. The money's yours!"

From the gathered crowd a number of expletives were issued.

"Son-of-a-bitch, I just lost twenty bucks," someone grumbled"

"What?" from another table, "Me too!"

"Only twenty," voiced someone from another table. "I gave the old fart 3:1 odds that Shirley's wouildn't dare him to do it—I just lost sixty dollars!" On and on it went around the crowded room.

"I'm old boys—not stupid." Vincent waved, as he stepped down from the podium to make the rounds and collect his winnings. True to his word, Vincent was definitely not stupid. As he passed the now re-composed secretary he said, "Here Shirley. Here's another twenty bucks for helping me out—one last time!"

A bad hair day!

Ted was a good looking officer who made a positive impression in both uniform and mufti (military-speak for ordinary clothes). With his straw-blond hair, steely-blue eyes, and pearly white goody-two-shoes grin, he could have been a male model. But Ted was a little, well—offbeat—if you know what I mean. No, he wasn't gay. He just did the bare necessities of the job and was the type of police officer who followed advice rather loosely. And orders? Well, some folk follow orders to the letter. Ted did not. Indeed, he seemed to follow them to the tune of a different orchestra. So everyone was surprised when he finally made Sergeant; and in charge of his own unit to boot! We all knew his promotion was due to longevity (also known as seniority) and that his downfall would come eventually.

One fine spring morning, the district commander called to say he was going to pay a casual "visit to the troops." Although "anti-establishment" and distinctly anti-headquarters, Ted still broke out into a cold sweat. He took to wiping his forehead with a Kleenex and keeping his arms by his sides so his co-workers couldn't spy his soaking armpits. One kind soul warned him to check a mirror and when he did he found his forehead covered with tiny pieces of tissue. We agreed afterwards that a lack of warning about the tissue might have made a pretty good prank in itself… but I digress.

When the commander arrived, Ted introduced us all and then invited the big-cheese into his personal office. Ted had made sure his desk was clean and orderly. His files were in order and we'd all been cautioned to have our uniforms in tip-top shape. Ted figured he had all the bases covered. The visit proceeded as well as planned; however, as the commander made ready to depart, he turned to Ted and said, "Pretty good Sergeant, just about everything seems to be in order."

"Just about everything?" asked Ted with a confused frown.

"Yup," countered the commander as he stared at Ted's shaggy mane of hair. "Everything's in order here except you! Just look at your hair! Good grief, check it out in a mirror Sergeant and do something about it, would you? You're setting a bad example for the rest of the officers!"

So Ted did something about it. The very next morning—after an early visit to a local hairdresser—he showed up with an enormous blond afro!

How to screw up a good joke

Eventually, I ended up serving in one of the regional headquarters of our esteemed institution of law enforcement. The work was less exciting than being on the street, but I enjoyed the nine-to-five hours and certainly didn't miss the drunks throwing up in the backseat of my police car. Life was good! At this particular headquarters, approximately one hundred civilian employees, sworn officers and medal encrusted "brass" filled an old three storey building on the outskirts of town. In such an insular environment, you can imagine how fast jokes make the rounds.

One Friday morning, I arrived for duty and slipped into our small cafeteria to enjoy an early cup of coffee with some of my colleagues. I told them a joke and we all laughed heartily. The joke went like this…

'A blind man walks into a local saloon with his seeing-eye dog. He gets comfortable at a stool at the bar and the bartender pours him a cold one. He sips his beer quietly. All of a sudden, he picks up his dog by the tail and swings it around wildly above his head.

"What the heck are you doing stranger?" asks the bartender.

"Oh—just looking around," the blind fellow replies.'

Okay, not a real a side-splitter, but my chums laughed anyway. Starting the day with a laugh or two never did anyone any harm.

As was often the case, the joke made the rounds of headquarters in record time. I was hardly surprised when another colleague tried to tell it back to me in the early afternoon while discussing a case of mutual interest.

After work that day, a few of us decided to celebrate the end of the week at a local police watering hole. After a few beers, in walked Allison. Now in all honesty, Allison was a wonderful person. She was pretty and outgoing, and was well liked by all and sundry. I guess only her hairdresser would have known for sure, but she was also a brunette. However, Allison should have been blond—if you get my drift.

"Hey guys," shouted Allison, "Have I ever got a joke for you! I just heard it this afternoon from one of the delivery guys at the loading dock. It goes like this…

> *"This good-old boy from the hills of Kentucky walks into a local saloon with his hunting dog. He gets comfortable at a stool at the bar and the bartender pours him a beer."*

A knowing glance passed amongst all present and a few of us smiled. Allison continued her story…

"All of a sudden, he picks up the mutt by the tail and starts swinging him around and around above his head."

Most of us were smiling by this time and a few had their heads turned to hide their giggling.

"'What in the Sweet Jesus are you doing?' asked the bartender." said Allison with a smile.

"'Oh, just looking around,' the hillbilly replied."

Upon concluding her joke, Allison burst into laughter and, without hesitation, so did the rest of us. In fact, most of us had been holding back and within a few seconds most of us had tears running down our cheeks and at least two burly officers were down on all fours hacking their guts out. Allison strutted down the length of the bar smiling proudly, obviously thinking... *Can I tell a joke or can I tell a joke?*

To this day, I don't think anyone had the heart to tell poor Allison why we were laughing so hard.

Be on the lookout for…

One thing cops pay attention to is an APB. This is, of course, the acronym for an "all-points-bulletin." When a dispatcher puts out a call on all frequencies to be on the lookout for a specific person or vehicle, we keep our eyes peeled and our senses on high alert. Such was the case one fine spring day when Reggie and I made an unannounced visit to the dispatch command center. Our request that morning was—a little out of the ordinary.

"I can't do that," the dispatcher said.

"Oh come on," Jean, my colleague begged. "The kid's on his first shift alone and is so full of piss & vinegar that we just gotta bring him down a notch or two. Heck,

Wyatt here's the "Officer of the Watch" so how much more authority do you need?

"Well, so long as the newbie can take a joke and this doesn't come back to haunt me," agreed Jean. "What about the other three cars out there, are they in on it?"

"Of course," confirmed Reggie with a snigger. "Okay Jean, do your thing!" Jean assumed her most serious dispatch-voice.

"Calling all cars, calling all cars; be on the lookout for a late model, four door Chevrolet, with licence plate XYZ 123. More info to follow as received."

"Great stuff, Jean," I said. "Just a little info at a time—it will drive the rookie crazy!" A few minutes later Jean made a second announcement.

"Calling all cars, calling all cars; update on earlier APB. The vehicle in question is now reported as being two-toned in color. Details still a little sketchy, but sounds like beige over dark brown or possibly white over dark blue or black." Our patrol cars at the time were commonly known as "black & whites." After another delay, Jean continued…

"Calling all cars, calling all cars; another update on that APB—the suspect vehicle has only one occupant—repeat, one occupant only. Subject is reported as being a white male in his early twenties with short blond hair and wearing a beige shirt or sweater with dark colored slacks or possibly jeans. Subject is not considered dangerous, but is wanted by Officers Jacobs and Holmes for unspecified reasons."

A few more minutes ticked merrily away on the dispatcher's wall clock as Reggie and I delivered Jean a hot coffee with double sugar and single cream; just the way she liked it. The double-chocolate dipped donut cemented her continued assistance.

"Calling all cars, calling all cars; on that APB, vehicle was spotted by foot patrol proceeding west on Main just past Church Street. Has anybody seen anything yet?"

The newbie, Officer Richards, promptly responded to Jean's enquiry.

"Dispatch, this is PC-29 heading east on Main Street. I just passed Church Street about two minutes ago. I didn't see it, but the suspect vehicle must have passed me going the other way just moments ago. Gee, I'm sorry dispatch, I'll swing around a make a pass westwards up Main Street a.s.a.p."

"Roger that, '29," replied Jean. "We just got another call from a citizen listening in on her police band radio and she says she thinks she saw the car pass through the parking lot next to Ernie's Auto Shop. The suspect may be casing the joint or something."

"Heck dispatch," responded PC-29, "I just went through there myself! He's gotta be close. Give me a couple of minutes and I'll have him tagged for sure!"

"Roger that '29,… uh—what? Well, are you sure? Uh, okay. Disregard earlier Roger, '29. I have new instructions for you. Please proceed direct to the squad room. The Officer of the Watch wants to speak to you!"

"Uh, okay. But I must be right on top of this cat. You sure the boss wants me to break it off right now?

"10-4, Officer Richards. The Officer of the Watch was very specific. He wants you here RIGHT NOW!"

"Acknowledged, dispatch. I'm on my way."

One couldn't help but hear Officer Richard's disappointment at having to break off his pursuit of the elusive suspect vehicle. One also couldn't help but hear the slight tremor in his voice. By this time he must have thought the Officer of the Watch was ready to ream him out for missing the APB'd vehicle not only once but twice in short order. As PC-29 drove into the office parking lot, Jean made her final announcement.

"Calling all cars, calling all cars. Disregard earlier APB. Vehicle has been sighted and sighting has been confirmed. In fact, the car's pulling into our parking lot right now. Subject of interest; yes, none other than our

Wyatt Holmes

own newbie officer, Carl Richards! That's right folks, Carl has just figured out that the black & white late model Chevy was his own pride and joy—PC-29. Guess he'll check his licence plate next time before going out on the road. Oh, Carl, if you were wondering what Jacobs & Holmes wanted you for—well, apparently you owe them a coffee and donut. In fact, Holmes just asked me to send you back out on the street to meet them at the donut shop at Fifth and Jefferson so you can pay up. If anyone else out there's in the mood for a free cup of java—Officer Richards is buying at Fifth and Jefferson. Did you copy all that '29.

"I copy that, dispatch," said Officer Richards with a laugh, "Thanks a bunch, Jean!"

Watch out for the dog!

When they attend a crime scene, police officers' senses go on high alert; especially when attending a serious crime scene. Sometimes an officer can get so wound up that his or her mind plays tricks on them.

Picture a rambling, two-storey rural farmhouse with a large barn and a couple of smaller outbuildings. Picture the adjacent fields full of dark rows of corn stalks and other hidden treasures of the soil. Picture a middle-aged uncle dead on the inside stairs of the farmhouse, a neat .22 calibre hole in the center of his neck— evidence of a violent death—but not, as it happens, the actual cause of death. Picture rather, Uncle Pete headfirst down the staircase, drowned in his own blood; a small trickle of which lies congealing in the folds of his corpulent neck. Picture Uncle Pete's fly open, stark support of his nephew's claim that he'd simply had enough of his uncle's many years of sexual abuse.

"He said we were going to play that dirty game again and I didn't know what else to do," said the traumatized nephew. "I warned him not to come up the stairs, but he wouldn't listen—so I grabbed Dad's rabbit gun and I shot him. I didn't mean to kill him—honest. I just wanted to scare him and get away."

By the time I got to the scene, the forensic investigators were hard at work in their white coveralls, masks, caps and paper booties. The senior investigator told me to check out the barn. As I sauntered across the farmyard he threw some casual advice over his shoulder…

"Wyatt, they apparently own a large dog which bolted when the old guy dropped on the stairs. It spends most of its time in the barn so be careful, it may still be a little spooked by all the ruckus."

"No problem, Harry," I replied.

The double-doors of the barn were ajar as I approached warily. Well, actually not too warily as the uncle-killer was sipping hot chocolate at the kitchen table and the only really bad guy on the property was already getting fitted for a custom made toe-tag. I looked back at Harry as I neared the open barn doors and shouted over my shoulder... "What type of dog is it anyway?"

"Don't know, Wyatt, all the kid said was that it's a big one!" Just then I heard a commotion from inside the barn. Suddenly, the doors flew open and out galloped a horse! Okay, more like a small pony! Yes, a pony! Not a dog—a pony! However, in the heat of the moment all I could see was a five-hundred pound, four foot high "dog" heading my way. I figured it was the *Hound of the Baskervilles* bound and determined to have me for supper!

Falling arse over tea-kettle backwards, I swivelled around and leap to safety as the pony galloped past me into the corn field. *Good riddance* was the first thing I thought as I got up and dusted myself off. The second thing I thought was whether or not Harry had seen me slip my pistol quietly back into its holster; 'cause if the damn "dog" had stopped for an instant his ass was grass and I was the lawn mower!

"Did you find the dog, Wyatt?" asked Harry, when I returned to the farmhouse.

"Nope, no dog in there—just a pony!" I replied, happy that no one appeared to have witnessed my quick draw McGraw act and ungainly backflip.

Quick Draw McGraw was a horse, wasn't he?

Oh yes, after all the dust settled, the nephew's own quick-draw actions were deemed to be "self-defence."

Licence and registration please!

Derek and I rarely worked together, but one night we were partnered up on the graveyard shift. Things were pretty quiet and we were aching for some action—any action. As we passed a local cemetery we noticed lights flashing on and off from behind a clump of trees in a local cemetery. We decided to investigate.

The lights were red, fairly bright, and blinked on and off in a fairly rhythmic manner. We parked our police car at the open cemetery gate and proceeded on foot with flashlights and batons at the ready.

"Could be grave robbers," offered Derek.

"Or maybe Satanic worshippers," I countered with a chuckle.

Out back of the trees and down a slight hill we spied an older model four-door Ford. Its brake lights were still flashing. As we crept closer, we noticed that the windows were all fogged up and that the car was rocking gently from side to side. Derek turned to me with a smile.

"I think these folk are worshipping something, but it sure as hell ain't the Devil."

As I stood at the left rear of the car, Derek opened the driver's door with a flourish. Inside, on the front seat, a young gentleman (and I use the term lightly) was straddled across a young "lady." Both were red in the face, sweating profusely, and naked as jaybirds!

"Would you exit the vehicle please Sir," said Derek seriously, somehow holding off a smile. The young lady grabbed what clothes she could to cover her dignity—very nice dignity I might add—while the young man jumped out and snapped to attention in front of us. He likely found the cool night air invigorating, but looked remarkably warm as he blushed from head to toe.

"May I see your driver's licence and registration please?" Derek recited in an officious monotone.

"Yes Sir, I have them right here," replied the young fellow and—as God is my witness—he whipped his right hand backwards and grabbed his right butt-cheek. However, the wallet he was searching for was still in the back pocket of his jeans on the floor of the Ford.

It was at that point that both Derek and I lost all composure. The young fellow gaped in surprise and relief at our laughter as Derek finished with, "Find another place to meet your girlfriend fella. We don't want you disturbing these kind folk in this their final resting place!"

'Yes Sir, officer," the boy replied sheepishly.

"Oh, one more thing," Derek offered, "In the future keep your foot off the brake pedal—it'll save us ALL a whole lot of trouble!"

"Oh bring back my body to me!"

In modern times, policing has become quite specialized with highly trained squads for drug enforcement, major crime investigations, K-9 patrol and many other areas of expertise. Thanks to TV shows and movies, one of the most recognized special sections is that of crime scene investigation or CSI. These are the guys and gals who show up in their pristine white jumpsuits and sterile booties to seal off a crime scene in an attempt to find fingerprints, identify physical matches, collect DNA and, of prime importance, take photographs.

Of course, when I was a young officer many jurisdictions didn't have the luxury of specialized squads and the rank and file did a little bit of everything. We were "jacks of all trades and masters of none," as they say. During our basic training we even received general instruction on how to contain; measure; and photograph a crime scene.

One day our office received a call from the Chief of a neighboring town to assist at the scene of a rather gruesome murder.

"We got this one pretty well wrapped up, Officer Holmes," I was told over the phone. "Crazy Billy-Bob Warburton finally went and did it—he finally done killed his wife!"

"That's terrible, Chief" I replied, "Crazy Billy-Bob's been a pressure cooker waiting to blow for many years now. Fortunately, Martha always seemed to know just how to calm him down—well—at least until today. How'd he do it?"

"He caught up to her in the barn with an axe! What a mess, there's blood everywhere and the regular crime scene guys are tied up with another case in the next county. They say they'll come on over eventually, but it'll be several hours before they arrive and we'd rather get this one over with, pronto-like!

"But it's a murder," I stammered, "What about the proper processing of the crime scene?"

"Not to worry young Wyatt. Billy-Bob called it in and met us at the barn door covered in blood. He then refused a lawyer and, after getting fully Miranda'ized—and we did it twice—he gave us a full confession.

"Sounds like you've got it nailed, Chief," I offered.

"Yup, knowing Billy-Bob's record, he'll plead guilty and be off to the penitentiary in lickity-split time! We even got his confession on tape using one of them new Dictaphone things. Yes-siree, we've got this one in the bag!"

"So what do you need from us?" I ventured.

"Well now Wyatt, although our department prides itself on being fully equipped, that new camera we bought last fall is on the fritz. It's the damnedest thing; we got rolls and rolls of film, just no camera to put 'em in!" he chuckled. Why don't you bring your camera over here and maybe we can all get home on time for supper!"

"I'll be right over!" I replied with a flourish. However, as I was pulling out our camera case from the storage locker—that's right, we only had one camera on hand in those days—my own boss showed up in one of his inquisitive moods.

"What're doing there, Wyatt?" he asked in a lazy drawl.

"Gotta get our camera over to Regina Falls pronto, Captain. They've got an open and shut murder case, but their camera's on the fritz so they need ours to take some crime scene photos."

"What about the CSI pros up in the capital?" he asked suspiciously. "You don't mean to tell me they're going to take their own photos at a murder scene? For crying out loud, that's why we've got that specialized squad, isn't it?"

"That's right, boss," but Chief Watson said they've got this one all wrapped-up except for a few photos; they even got the murderer's confession on tape! It's Crazy Billy-Bob Warburton and he's done killed his wife with an axe!"

"Okay Wyatt, but why don't you give me that camera? Your shift is about to end and Jane's at her mother's tonight, so I've got some spare time on my hands. I'll take the camera over to Regina Falls and maybe Ralph Watson'll invite me to supper. His Suzie is quite the cook, you know!"

So that's how I ended up heading for home and how my boss ended up carrying our camera case to Regina Falls.

It took a day or two for the truth to trickle out, as immediately after the fact "the thin blue line" circled the wagons to protect a couple of red-faced reputations. But you can't keep secrets forever, I guess.

As it happened, my boss showed up in Regina Falls to a warm welcome from Chief Watson. He whipped out our camera from its case and promptly screwed it on to the fancy six-D-cell flash attachment we'd just purchased a few weeks earlier. My boss almost blinded Chief Watson as he snapped about twenty pictures. He knew that we only bought rolls of film good for thirty-six photos so he was confident of not running short of celluloid. He also knew that extra rolls were in the camera case and, in any event, Regina Falls had lots of film—just no camera!

"Okay boys," shouted Chief Watson to the ambulance attendants, "She's all yours!" The two burly drivers carefully placed Martha Warburton into an oversized black body-bag and with as much respect as they could muster, carried her out to the ambulance for transportation to the morgue. Just as the twin-doors closed with sober finality, my boss uttered a strangled cry.

"Damn it Ralph, but we got a problem buddy!"

"What problem, Hank?"

"Well, I just went to change the roll of film and there ain't none in this here camera—no roll of film, that is. I guess that darn boy, Wyatt, forgot to load the camera before he gave it to me! What're we gonna do now?"

"Hold that ambulance, boys!" shouted Chief Watson over his shoulder. "We need the body back in the barn for photos—pronto!"

"What! You can't do that, Ralph," my boss whispered frantically. "This is, after all a murder scene!"

"Oh, so you'd rather show up at the inquest with no photos and have to explain how a bunch of country bumpkins like us fouled up a murder scene?"

"Uh, no—not exactly; but... but," stammered my boss.

"No if and or buts about it, Henry," continued Chief Watson, "It ain't gonna be pretty, but it's gotta be done."

"BRING HER BACK BOYS! That's right, Martha! Just bring the lady back and reposition her the way you found her in the barn."

Needless to say, all involved were sworn to secrecy. Truth be told, it made not a bit of difference to the eventual outcome. Billy-Bob did indeed plead guilty and did indeed head off to the penitentiary for a lengthy stay.

I, of course, escaped any criticism because as all involved knew full well— even the two chiefs—one never loaded film into a police camera until actually at the crime scene. It's one of the basic rules of crime scene photography. It's so that one is assured of having fresh film and also so no one makes the dumb mistake of… well, you get the picture!

Suicide? Murder? Suicide?

One day we were called to the scene of what, on initial examination, looked like just one more routine sudden death—a suicide. On arrival at a large home on the outskirts of town we were met by a teenage boy in obvious distress.

"Grandpa's in his workshop. I think he's dead."

On entering the workshop, which was actually more like a small barn, we found an elderly gentleman hanging quietly from the central roof-truss. A rough noose encircled his neck and yes, he was dead—definitely dead; believe me, you don't want to know the details.

Investigational procedures vary in direct relation to the seriousness of the situation. As this was obviously a self-inflicted death, we decided not to call in any CSI assistance. As a result, neither photographs nor detailed measurements of the scene were taken. We called the local coroner who authorized the removal of the body. As a routine precaution, the coroner also authorized an autopsy. A couple of hours later, we received a request from the hospital to call the senior pathologist—STAT!

"Hi Doc," my partner Bill commenced, "You wanted to talk to us about that old gent we found hanging around in his garage?" He listened to the physician for a moment and then said, "Whadda you mean, Doc. Don't start jiving us—that ain't funny in the least." I noticed at this point that Bill's knuckles were white where they'd tightened around the phone. More listening followed and then, "Uh, well, you see; it looked so obviously like a suicide we never called those guys in." By now Bill's knuckles were ghostly white – almost translucent even. Again, more listening, then Bill hung up after saying, "We're on it Doc, thanks!"

"What was all that about," I asked Bill. In reply he repeated both sides of the conversation to me as follows…

Doc: *"Hanging around? Ah yes, police humor I suppose. Well, the old gent you 'found hanging around' as you put it was probably already dead before he started swinging."*

Bill: *"Whadda you mean, Doc? Don't start jiving us – that ain't funny in the least."*

Doc: *"I wish I was 'jiving you,' as you say, but this particular gent has five distinct skull fractures which, in my opinion, represent five separate blows to the head with a blunt instrument. My guess is a baseball bat or axe handle as I also found several splinters of wood in his scalp; perhaps oak or ash— I can't be sure without further forensic tests. What did the crime scene investigators find? Has the major crime team started interviewing the family and any neighbors to identify motive and opportunity?*

Bill: *"Uh, well, you see; it looked so obviously a suicide we never called those guys in."*

Doc: *"What! Well, you'd better correct that error lickity-split officer, or your Captain just may decide to put you back on permanent night patrol, starting this evening!"*

Bill: *"We're on it Doc, thanks!"*

"Wyatt," Bill managed to squeak out to me, "We've got some back-tracking to do and we've got to do it NOW! You call in CSI and I'll go beg a favour from the major crime guys. Oh yeah, and give that kid a call and tell him not to touch anything in his grandfather's workshop. Better yet, get down there yourself with a couple of other guys and secure the scene. Hell and damnation, only three years to retirement and this has to jump up and bite me in the butt!"

Well, by the end of the day CSI had done their thing and by the end of the next day the major crime investigators had also finished. Bill and I got called in to meet with Lt. Fowler, the head of the major crime unit. We figured our goose was cooked.

"Hi boys," he started with a smirk. "Guess this one kinda got away from you initially." We replied with silence as we figured there was more to come. "Well, it seems it's your lucky day after all."

"Our lucky day?" gasped Bill.

"Yup, after many hours by some of my top investigators, we've confirmed this one to be—just as you called it on day-one—a suicide."

"A suicide?" both Bill and I said at the same time.

"How can that be," I asked, "The guy had five skull fractures—it can't be a suicide!"

"Oh yes it can," replied Lt. Fowler. "Your only mistake was not checking the noose more closely. You see, he hung himself—with a bungee cord!"

The last story is, of course, just an old joke
I heard many years ago and which I've
used many times while sharing a beer
or two with unsuspecting friends. I
apologize for leading you along, but it
does have the requisite elements of a
humorous crime story and I thought it might
be a good way to wrap up this little tome of
police-related anecdotes.

Wyatt

CPSIA information can be obtained at www.ICGtesting.com
Printed in the USA
LVOW05s0347100314

376641LV00003B/76/P

9 780988 590298